J. R.

MW01015761

Other Buck Logan Suspense Novels by
J.R. Stoddard

COUGAR HUNT

Enjoy

J.R. Stoddard

COUGAR CAMP

COUGAR CAMP

By

J.R. STODDARD

A Buck Logan Suspense Novel

Cougar Publishing

COUGAR CAMP

To Lois Roberta Stoddard
1921-2000
My loving mother who, along with my father, taught
me the wonders of nature through numerous
camping, fishing, hunting and hiking trips.

J. R. STODDARD

Newtown is a fictional town, as are all the characters in this book.

COUGAR CAMP

Copyright © 2004 by J.R. Stoddard
Library of Congress Control
Number: 2004092088
ISBN: 0-9701401-3-4

Cougar pictures by Lee Dygert

Cougar drawing by Robert E. Stoddard (Son)

Cover Design by Kathy Campbell

FIRST EDITION, July 2004

Cougar Publishing
Olympia, Washington

Published in the United States of America

Many thanks to my loving wife and best friend of twenty-six years for all of her proofing and editing. Thanks also to Mary Baker for proofreading and providing ideas.

J. R. STODDARD

COUGAR CAMP

Drawing by Robert E. Stoddard (Son)

1

The small Cessna 172 airplane glided smoothly through the air on a clear, crisp afternoon. In the distance, closer to the Cascade Mountains, they could see a few puffs of silver lined clouds. The engine hummed along with a low, slightly labored sound as Eric adjusted the prop pitch. Inside the cockpit it was a bit cool because the heater was not putting out enough heat for the high altitude, but the ski jackets kept them comfortably warm. Eric scanned the instruments; flaps up, airspeed had decreased to fifty knots. Pulling back gently on the yoke the nose of the aircraft began to rise as it tried, in vain, to climb. Airspeed quickly fell off and the yoke soon began to shake in his hands, gently at first, then becoming more pronounced. Not something a pilot could miss, much less ignore. Soon the yoke progressed into a fierce shake and the whole aircraft began to vibrate. The aircraft shudder went quickly from a shake into a violent vibration. Eric put in a little right rudder as the aircraft tried to fall off to the left. Then the engine stalled.

Quickly, he pushed the yoke well forward allowing the nose to float downward before he lost control of the aircraft. The prop began to spin again and he reached over to the prop control and increased the pitch and throttle. After falling about one thousand feet the engine caught and he leveled off the aircraft at six thousand feet.

"Good job," Buck said, "that was smoothly done. I think we've had enough stall practice for today. Let's head back to Arlington field."

Buck's son, Eric, had expressed an interest in flying when he was fifteen years old. He wanted to follow in his father's footsteps and be a pilot. It wasn't until he was seventeen that he exhibited that intense interest, a fire in his eyes to learn to fly. Buck knew that in order to be successful you had to really want it. Learning to fly took intelligence, the capacity to learn quickly, the ability to understand very complex mechanical and electrical systems, and usually an aggressive success-oriented individual with no fear. Today would be his second one-hour lesson in a Cessna 172.

"OK," as he turned to a heading of two two zero and began to descend.

"Arlington this is Cessna 14372. We're on your zero four zero at twenty-five miles, VFR descending through four thousand for two thousand five hundred. Inbound for a full stop."

"Cessna 14372 this is Arlington Field, roger, we have you on radar. Wind 270 at ten knots, ceiling five thousand, visibility five miles. Report at the initial approach fix."

"Cessna 14372, wind 270 at ten, wilco."

Eric could see the field now and turned left to intercept the initial approach fix. He finished the approach checklist, and went through the before landing checklist. At four hundred feet above the ground he lowered the flaps for the final approach. Decreasing the airspeed he passed over a fence at the approach end of the runway and lowered the nose a little more until the two main wheels touched the asphalt. As the plane continued down the runway he held the yoke back until the nose wheel made contact and gave him steering wheel direction control.

Taxiing off the active runway back to the hangar Buck proudly said, "Fine landing Eric."

When Swawa, the Indian name for cougar, left Cross Point she zigzagged through the forests of the northern Cascades in search of a home range area of her own. She needed to find an area that did not already have a resident cougar. On the second day out she came across a pile of cougar scat that had been partly covered with twigs and urine, indicating another cougar had already staked out the area. She continued on, making her way through a forest of old growth trees. On the fourth night she slept in a huge old cedar tree. The branch she selected was over twenty inches in diameter, and about ten feet above the ground, it was also the closest to the ground. At five-thirty in the morning she was startled out of a deep slumber when a bird, directly below her on the ground, belted out its song. A mist hung heavy in the cool morning air. The robins had returned to the northwest. The red breasted bird searched around in the grass at the base of the tree, singing its loud, high-pitched song again. Swawa's attention was totally focused, breakfast had arrived.

After watching the robin for about a minute, judging its movements, she glided silently, and effortlessly out of the tree. The bird was intent on its search for worms, but sensing something was wrong, it opened its wings, flexed its legs and jumped into the air. Only inches above the ground Swawa's right front paw landed directly on top of the robin, pressing it to the ground. She curled her paw and extended her claws impaling the robin, insuring her meal wouldn't get away. She held the bird down with her left paw and used the right paw to pull off the wings. Deftly peeling off the skin with her razor sharp claws, she made a quick meal of the bird. Not much of a meal for a cougar, but a nice snack. Lying stretched out on the ground at the base of the tree licking her paws she heard other robins singing. The songs were coming from all directions.

She crouched down and easily jumped back up to her branch. Cougars can jump more than twenty feet straight up into a tree from a standstill position. She lay back down on her branch and patiently waited. Within ten minutes there was another robin in the grass below her tree, looking for worms. She repeated this new hunting tactic five times that morning. If necessary, five birds can satisfy a young cougar's appetite for a whole day. More importantly, she was honing her hunting skills.

Swawa had been fortunate to find a territory within weeks of the time she had departed the Cross Point area near Newtown. It was unusual for an area so abundant in elk and deer to be uninhabited by a predator. When a juvenile cougar leaves its mother it is critical for it to find and claim its own territory. Sometimes cougars will traverse over other predator's territory for years before finding one of their own. Their chances of long-term survival are remote without a permanent territory of their own. The more frequently a cougar must go through another predator's territory, in search of its own territory, the greater the chances of an altercation. A young cat isn't as experienced as the more mature inhabitant, consequently there is a greater likelihood of the transient being killed and eaten.

Normally female cougars won't mate until after they have claimed their own territory. It is fairly common for a female's territory to be bordered by two different male's territory on opposite sides, with overlapping borders.

Not long after Swawa secured her own home range she went into heat. Her bloodcurdling screams, to attract a mate, went on for three nights before two male suitors arrived, at the same time. Both of the males were big, strong, mature adults. One weighed about one hundred forty pounds, the other over one hundred sixty pounds. Swawa backed away to the side as the two males sized each other up, pacing from side to side. They began to spar around in a circle, eyeing each other with fierce determination.

Suddenly, the slightly larger one attacked with lightning fast speed lunging at the upper part of his opponent's right front leg. He got a solid bite, sinking his long canine teeth deep into the muscle tissue of his opponent. The opponent was ready for the attack, lashing out with his right front paw slashing its claws into the upper shoulder, but the purchase was fleeting, as the bigger cat twisted around, dislodging it. The forest was filled with the smaller cat's desperate screams as it struggled to get a biting grip on the bigger cat that was quickly overpowering him.

Besieged, he was unable to maintain a hold on the bigger cat, either with his fangs or his claws. Struggling and twisting it tried to free itself, but the larger male held fast with his jaws firmly attached. Taking his right front paw, the bigger cat sunk his claws deep into the opposite shoulder. His powerful jaws ripped a chunk of meat out of the leg and then quickly lunged back at the neck, securing a strangle hold on the side of his opponent's throat.

Thrashing around, the smaller cat screamed out in pain, its legs flailing, trying to get his claws into his attacker. Lifting the smaller cat by the neck the attacker was able to pin him to the ground. Quickly, thrusting his hind leg claws, the larger cat violently forced its claws into the soft underside of his opponent's belly. Finishing the attack, by using its powerful muscles, he thrust his leg down, disemboweling the younger cat. In the world of predators, the lack of experience often precludes the young from living long enough to mate.

Spent from the massive effort, the bigger cat lay motionless watching his opponent desperately try to crawl off, dragging his entrails, within minutes he stopped, eyes fading closed as the involuntary muscles spasms began to twitch. The victor licked his wounds, but it didn't take long for the scent of the female's pheromones to gain control of his senses again and revive his interest. Languorously, he got up and went over to Swawa. She was impressed at his prowess, as he licked her neck, and didn't repel his amorous advance.

After resting they both went over to the dying opponent and began to feed. For the next three days they mated twenty to thirty times a day. By the end of the third day Swawa had conceived and the carcass of the defeated opponent was nearly consumed. Her mission accomplished, she became aggressive, chasing her suitor away.

Ninety days later Swawa had five kittens, an unusually large number of kittens for a young cougar's first litter. A female cougar will come into her first heat at twenty-six to thirty months old. Normally, a female cougar will have one or two kittens for her first litter. Swawa's first litter of five was extraordinary, and probably attributable to the abundance of food she had been able to kill for months before she conceived. When there is an abundance of food for wild animals it stimulates the ovaries to produce more eggs and results in larger litters. For most animals it also produces more frequent litters.

Cougars are antisocial creatures with a voracious appetite for meat. When male cougars meet in the wild it frequently ends with one cougar killing the other, the victor making a meal of the looser. This cannibalistic behavior is common among male cougars. With females it is sometimes different. Overlapping female territories occasionally result in chance encounters, but they seem to tolerate each other better, and these meetings do not always end in battle.

Over a year had passed since Swawa left her mother and siblings from the Cross Point area in search of her own territory. She lay on the grass in the shade under an old cedar tree with her five juvenile offspring. Her kittens were now eight months old, ranging in weight from sixty-five to eighty pounds each. She had trained them how to hunt and survive on their own. For the first four months Swawa had killed a deer about every four days, the meat kept her milk supply plentiful enough to feed her kittens. When the kittens were four months old they began to eat meat and they all started to hunt together. Swawa trained them how to hunt and they grew quickly, especially one of the males. As the kittens grew they began to eat more meat, the six of them needed to kill a deer or small elk nearly every day to provide enough for all of them to eat. By the time the kittens were eight months old they had killed over one hundred ungulates in Swawa's home range, along with numerous other small animals; raccoons, possums, squirrels and rabbits. There were still animals in the area, but the population density of prey animals was now so low that finding enough for the six of them was becoming increasingly difficult.

The kittens had grown quickly because of the initial high food supply. Before 1990 kittens would stay with the mother for about twenty-four months before being ready to go out on their own. Initially the abundant food supply caused the kittens to grow fast, but when the food supply was diminished the mother would be forced to disperse the kittens at a younger age than normal, to keep them all from starving. Under these circumstances, this tends to happen when the kittens are about eight months old. With a continuous abundant food supply a female could produce five times the number of offspring she would have during a time when food was not so plentiful.

Doug and Andy sat in the little café drinking coffee and eating a bowl of the day's special, 'Spotted Owl soup.' Actually it was creamed chicken but aptly named for a town that previously had been heavily dependent on the logging industry. Both were loggers who were lucky if they were able to get one load of logs to haul per week. The controversy that logging had caused the spotted owl to be put on the endangered species list had bankrupt both of them. They both had attended a community college for over two years on a state sponsored program for displaced workers. They'd both received an Associate of Arts degree in business. The state and the entire country were in a severe economic recession. For men over fifty, who had never done anything but logging their whole life, there was no hope of any other employment in the small northwest college town. As they looked out the window a man, probably in his late thirties, caught their attention within ten minutes of his arrival at the corner. They'd lived in the town all their lives and were accustomed to seeing all kinds of people and nationalities around town, but they could tell immediately that this one was different. He just stood there on the corner, looking at all the cars as they drove past. Within thirty minutes a car pulled up to the curb and the man went over to the car, talking to the driver through the passenger window. In a few minutes he pulled something out of his pocket and handed it to the girl in the car. She in turn handed him something and then sped off down the street.

Doug and Andy sat there observing him for about an hour. Doug commented, "Looks like we've got another one of them drug dealers from California."

"Yep. This one looks a bit older than the others."

"Guess it's been about three months since the last one showed up. They must have some kind of cycle or something," Doug answered. "I suppose we'd better take him for a ride after it gets dark."

"Uh huh." They continued to sit and watch.

Doug's son had died from a drug overdose when he was seventeen years old. Andy had caught his daughter smoking marijuana behind the garage one afternoon. He gave her a severe thrashing and sent her to her room. The next morning they found a note on her bed that said, 'There's too many rules for me to stay here any longer.' She ran away at the age of fourteen and turned to prostitution to survive. She soon got into heavy drugs, and was now in jail for robbery, a result of trying to support a heavy drug habit. Andy and his wife went to visit her at least once a week, in hope that she would come home when she got out of jail so they could help her get her life back together. The men were committed to ridding the streets of drug dealers.

Buck and Eric walked into the little café after their flight and saw Bull Towns and another man sitting at a booth.

Bull recognized Buck and Eric right away and waved them over to their table.

"Hi Bull, mind if we join you folks?" Buck asked.

Bull and Rick both motioned for them to sit down.

Bull said, "Buck and Eric, this is Rick, we're old friends. Rick's a forest ranger and he's back in town for a few days."

Buck and Eric both replied "Hi, nice to meet you."

"I saw you had a plane reserved for this fine afternoon. How'd the flight go?" asked Bull.

"Great," Eric said with a big smile on his face, "we practiced stalls and did a few touch and goes."

"That's a good thing to do early on," Bull said. He was the owner of the flying school at the small airfield on the edge of town and it was one of his airplanes they had rented.

"Yeah, it was a fantastic day to go flying. It was so clear we could see all the way to the islands," Buck said.

Buck ordered coffee, Eric a soda, and both got a slice of apple pie, Eric's a-la-mode. While they ate they all talked about flying and the weather for half an hour. Buck and Eric announced it was time to get going and said good-bye. Buck paid the bill and as they were walking out they passed Doug and Andy, who were intently studying the man across the street.

It looked like things were finally coming together. Uri Kasboff had left mother Russia over three months ago. Russia was a disaster. Life had been good when he was a KGB officer. Other people could barely find enough to eat, but he had just about anything he wanted. Good food, women and vodka were always available.

The early nineties changed all that when Russia came apart after the cold war ended. All of a sudden he was unemployed, within six months he was living on the streets. About a year later the foreigners began to arrive, they wanted a piece of the action in Russia's new economy, Americans, Germans and Japanese, all carrying big wads of cash. His KGB training was exactly what he needed. Shadowing the foreigners gave him the chance to observe their habits. It was easy, they were so busy flashing their wealth around they never suspected a tail. He almost laughed out loud at the ease of monitoring the foreigners. He developed a plan, one which he would use over and over.

His first attempt in carrying out the plan was almost a disaster. Watching the American he had staked out for the last three days he soon learned his habits. He would leave the bar at eleven each night, in a state of intoxication, and make his way back to the hotel. Uri went ahead of the American, entered the hotel and waited for him at the end of the hall. The timing was perfect. As soon as the man exited the elevator, Uri appeared to be just walking toward his own room, timing it so that he was abreast of the man as he put the key into the door to his room. Uri slipped the garrote over his head, but before he could tighten it around his thick neck the man, apparently not as intoxicated as he assumed, whipped around, catching him by surprise. A scuffle ensued, Uri kneed him in the groin, but the only effect it seemed to have was making the man angry and mad as hell. The man bent down thrusting his head into Uri's mid section. Pressed against the wall Uri kneed the man under the chin causing the American to stumble to an upright position. He quickly gave the soft businessman a powerful punch in the solar plexus. When he bent over in pain Uri judo chopped the back of his neck with all his might using both hands clasped together, dropping him to the floor in a limp pile. He hadn't realized that he'd lost some of his strength and finesse in the past year. The attack was sloppy and could have brought the attention of other hotel guests, but luck was on his side. Uri pushed the door open and dragged the man into the room, kicked the door closed, slipped the garrote back over his head and pulled it tight to finish the job holding it long enough to ensure the man was dead.

Uri went through the man's pockets, removing the wallet and a stack of cash that was hidden in a compartment of his jacket pocket. Quickly he put everything that was valuable or could contain anything valuable into the suitcase and walked out of the hotel into a dark, rainy night. He stole off to a secluded place in a derelict old building where he knew no other homeless street people would bother him. Piece by piece he examined everything thoroughly, finding over a thousand dollars in cash and a handful of credit cards. Confidently, he knew the few police left in town would never find out who did it. When the hotel staff discovered the body tomorrow the police would be summoned. On arrival they'd look at the scene, make out a report, and that would be the end of the investigation. The body would be turned over to the American Embassy.

During the next five years he killed four Americans, two Germans, and one Japanese. After his first encounter he'd learned not to make mistakes. It was so simple. He used a sap, a small leather sack filled with tiny lead pellets that had a loop on one end, to knock the man out as he entered the room, and the garrote to finish the job. He was living even better than he had been before the economy collapsed. He used the credit cards to pay rent six months in advance, stocked up on food, bought cases of vodka, and got cash for several months before the credit cards stopped working. Over time the foreigners slowly stopped coming. It had been many months since he'd seen a foreigner. Word had gotten out that it was a dangerous place. No way did he want to be desperate and on the streets again. Now that the government didn't restrict travel he could go anywhere he wanted. He'd heard America was the place to go and easy to get in if you knew how to do it.

Uri bribed a deck hand to hide him on a ship to Canada. Russia was shipping furniture to Canada. It was poor quality workmanship, but it was cheap, so it sold well. When they arrived at the huge Port of Vancouver, British Columbia, Uri slipped unnoticed through customs inside a large cherry wood cabinet. In the middle of the night Uri extricated himself from the cabinet and container, and headed for the lights of town.

Within two days in the huge city of Vancouver he located someone to make him a fake Washington driver's license, but it cost him more than he expected. Down to one hundred US dollars, he took a bus from town to the border where the U.S. customs agent asked a lot of questions because of his accent. Impatient to enter the United States, he knew to be careful, not wanting his accent to be so obvious. His KGB training had taught him much about the United States, including the English language. When the US border agent began asking him questions he said that he had been in Vancouver for three days vacationing and that he was born in Seattle. The agent asked about his accent and Uri told him his parents were Russian emigrants and they had kept him out of school because they were illegal, but he was American born and therefore a citizen of the United

States. The customs agent turned to his computer and looked up the name and address. The guy that had made his phony drivers license apparently knew what the agent would check. The agent said he was free to continue on his way. Uri walked out of the office and gave a sigh of relief, heading south into Washington State without looking back.

By the time he arrived in the northwest college town he only had fifty dollars left. Not enough to have a motel room and eat too. It would take some time to figure out where he would get more money. The first night he spent in town at the Salvation Army's shelter for homeless people. It was an acceptable place to stay for a night or two, a hot meal and a warm bed. The problem was the other people there, he just didn't like them. It was too crowded and full of mental problems. Uri had been a loner for some time now. He scouted around the small town and found a building on the college campus with a boiler room in the basement. The ground next to the building was warm and there was even an overhang above to keep the rain away. Liberating a sleeping bag from the shelter, he spent the nights lying next to the building. During the day he'd found something else he was looking for, food. He watched the small café in the evenings. At precisely nine, the cook came out and threw away the garbage. Uri waited until a little after the café closed at ten and then scoured the small dumpster, finding discarded rolls and occasionally an unopened loaf of bread. That was all he needed for now, bread and a bottle of vodka every day. The vodka was so expensive in America, he only had enough money left for a few days.

Not knowing exactly what he was looking for at first, he felt he would know immediately when he saw it. He walked around the small town at various hours of the day and night, observing everything. When he rounded the corner in town, near the college, the young Asian, probably a Vietnamese, was standing there with his boom box tuned to the local rock station. It struck Uri immediately that he was selling drugs. He'd been to Vietnam many times when he was a KGB officer. He was stationed in Petropavlovsk, a beautiful seaport city near the tip of the Kamckatka peninsula on the north east coast of Russia. In the eighties he'd been an advisor when Hanoi was trying desperately to get its finances in order after the war. The Soviets had taken an even bigger stake in the communist country after the U.S. pulled out of South Vietnam in the 70's. He observed the dealer all day from a distance. Around midnight the dealer got into a black late model two door Toyota that was parked nearby. Uri quickly memorized the license plate number. Early the next morning he walked around the small town until he found the late model black Toyota parked at a cheap motel. It was in front of a room at the end of the building, well away from the office, just what he'd hoped for. He wasn't sure about taking the man at a motel though. America might be different from what he was accustomed to, and the old plan might not work here. He thought about it, the man seemed more vulnerable at times standing alone out on the street in the dark.

The next day while he was walking around the town he found a piece of nylon rope, about two feet long, and a plastic broom handle. He cut off two, four inch sections from the broom handle and attached the ends of the rope to the plastic pieces. Late that night, about the time the man usually left, Uri sneaked around the building and quietly snuck up behind the dealer. He had a twenty-four ounce can of beer in his hand and an empty one was on the sidewalk next to him. Apparently his senses were dulled because he was unaware of Uri's presence. Uri slipped the rope around the stranger's neck, crossed his arms and twirled around, placing his back up against the back of the dealer. Lifting him off the ground he headed behind a building, out of sight. The dealer reached over his head, clawing at Uri, trying to get a grip on his attacker. Uri held fast moving behind the building quickly, the dealer's arms and legs twisting in the air. When the dealer went limp he held on for another minute, then dropped him to the ground. He took the keys out of the dealers pocket, pulled the car up next to the body and loaded it in the trunk of the car. Then he drove to the small café and parked the car in the rear of the building next to the dumpster. It was now just after two in the morning and there were no people to be seen anywhere. He got out and looked around to ensure that he was not being watched,

opened the trunk and cleaned everything out of the
dealer's pockets. There was over a thousand dollars in
cash. Placing the body in the dumpster, he covered it
up with trash. Glad he'd done his homework, he
could walk away without concerns of being caught.
The trash was picked up at the small café around six
o'clock on Tuesday mornings.

Over five thousand dollars in cash, four boxes of
drugs, marijuana, crack, and some meth in various
size bags were found at the dealer's motel room.
When he finished loading it all into the car he drove
to the other side of town and rented a cheap motel by
the week. Now he had enough money to live
comfortably for months, but he needed a plan. Drugs,
easy to sell, were worth a small fortune and he had no
problem with selling them. He'd observed the dealer
for a few days and figured he could make some extra
money, the customers already knew where to go.

He caught a few hours of sleep and headed back
to the small cafe at five thirty. He parked the car
about a block away where he could see the dumpster.
If the body was discovered it could be a problem, he'd
want to get out of town before the police started an
investigation. The refuse truck arrived at six ten,
extending the fork under the dumpster, the driver
lifted it and the lid flew open as the contents fell into
the back of the truck. The driver banged the fork up
and down twice to dislodge anything that might be
stuck, then returned the dumpster to its resting place.
Pulling out of the parking lot onto the main road the

driver pressed the lever to compact the newly collected refuse. Satisfied he was safe so far, Uri went back to the motel and went to bed.

The refuse truck continued on its collection rounds until it was too full to compact any more. At five after ten he pulled into the line of trash trucks waiting at the landfill to dump their loads. Ten minutes later he backed up to the dumping point, lifted the handle for the hydraulic system to lift the front of the load bed, then pressed another button to open the rear door. The load slid out in a mighty rush of noise and odors. The rats scurried out of the way only long enough for the commotion to stop. The driver pulled away slowly, lowering the load bed as he drove. The next truck executed a similar maneuver. None of the drivers got out of their trucks. The only person around was the bulldozer driver. After two more trucks dumped their loads the dozer moved in and pushed the odiferous heap of mostly big plastic bags up onto the major pile, which grew about ten feet a day. The rats scattered to avoid being crushed as the huge blade pushed tons of trash, the heavy steel tracks mashing everything underneath. The sun, while not a hot day, still heated the moldering mass, speeding up the process of decay. Rats numbered in the thousands, some as big as house cats.

The following afternoon Uri stood on the corner listening to the boom box the dealer used when he was doing business. He assumed it must be part of the way to draw his customers in.

A new song came on, "I'm goin'a be rich, lots and lots of money," the radio blared away. That's right he thought as he listened, in only four hours he'd sold enough baggies of grass to cover expenses for a week. No crack or meth had sold yet, but it wouldn't be long before it started to move. Once it got dark business really picked up. The word spread fast around campus in a small town like this.

Doug and Andy looked out the window in the direction of the university. The tall evergreens cast long shadows as the horizon turned orange and slowly changed to darkness. Doug and Andy walked out of the café and Doug got into his pick-up. Andy walked around the corner and up the street, crossed over and started walking toward the dealer. Doug, who had a heavy beard, drove slowly down the street, stopped at the curb, and rolled down the window.

"Hey dude," he asked, "got any weed?"

"Weed, where you from man? Nobody calls it weed any more," but he was new here and wasn't familiar with the customs yet, as Uri assessed the man. He looked like one of them old hippies he'd seen in the papers years ago when the students were protesting the Vietnam War. He leaned slightly against the cab of the truck and looked inside, checking it out and thinking this guy looks too old, but maybe that's why he calls it weed.

Andy was quietly walking past and got Uri's attention. He turned around to check him out, but Andy just sidled on unobtrusively not paying any attention to the Russian. When Uri turned back to his customer he found himself looking down the barrel of a .45 caliber semi-automatic pistol. At the same time he felt a push in the middle of his back as Andy pressed his hand down on the bulge of the 9mm Uri had appropriated from the Asian dealer, tucked in the back of his waist-band. Simultaneously he felt the muzzle of a .45 at the base of his skull. Andy removed the dealer's 9mm.

"What does this mean?" Startled at this change of events and upset with himself for being so careless.

"Put both hands behind your back."

"What is this?" as he did what he was told, looking at each of them, one at a time, for an opportunity to grab one of their guns and take control of the situation.

"Shut up," Doug barked waving the .45 at Uri while Andy put a plastic garbage bag tie around both wrists, like a pair of handcuffs, and cinched it up as tight as it would go.

"Hey, that hurts. You can't do this. I've got rights. This is America."

In one motion, Andy grabbed Uri's chin, pulled his mouth open and stuffed in an old dirty sock, opened the door and pushed him in. Andy looked at the man, thinking he looked a little old for a drug dealer. The others had always been much younger and were always Asian or black. As soon as Andy got in, Doug quickly pulled away. Andy ripped off a piece of duct tape and slapped it over Uri's mouth, then pulled a pillowcase over his head.

They drove up into the north Cascade Mountains about two hours away to a remote place they knew well. Being loggers they were familiar with just about every old dirt road in the isolated mountainous area. The odds of this guy finding his way back from such a secluded area were not in his favor.

Doug brought the truck to a stop when they arrived at their usual drop off spot. Andy grabbed Uri by the arm, pulled him out, shoving him in front of the truck, with the hi-beams shining on him. Andy pulled the pillowcase off and ripped the tape from his mouth, tearing away a fair amount of skin off his lips along with it. Uri spit out the sock and yelled from the pain. Andy then cut the plastic tie off his wrists and walked around to the side of the truck where Uri couldn't see him because of the blinding light from the headlights. Doug and Andy stood on opposite sides of the truck with their guns trained on Uri.

"Take off your clothes and throw them over here," Andy demanded.

"Are you nuts, what's going on here?" as Uri stood there waving his arms all around in the air, "I'm not taking my clothes off out here in the middle of nowhere. Are you some kind of perverts?"

Doug fired a .45 round right between Uri's legs, high enough to create a substantial wind current around his genitals. They were in control and he was not seeing any opportunity to change that.

"OK, OK," as he hastily began removing his clothes.

"Everything, the shoes and socks too," said Doug.

Andy picked up all the clothes and got back into the truck while Doug kept the .45 trained on Uri. While Doug got into the truck Andy rolled down his window.

"We've got a nice, quiet, law abiding little town and we intend to keep it that way. I suggest you don't come back. If you show up there again we won't be as friendly next time."

It was a cold evening, at an elevation of over four thousand feet. Andy rolled up his window as they drove off down the gravel road. Then he turned the fan on to high and slid the heat control knob over to full warm.

The sharp stones immediately began to cut Uri's feet as he started walking down the gravel road.

"Friendly? Friendly? You call this friendly? This is bullshit man. If this is northern hospitality I don't need any more of this shit!" Uri screamed, waving his fist around in the air at the departing pick-up truck, now well out of hearing range. He was used to the cold, being from Pertopavlosk. Under the circumstances, with no clothes, he knew he was in big trouble.

About ten miles down the road Doug and Andy drove over a bridge. The river was far below. Doug stopped the truck in the middle of the bridge while Andy went through the pants pockets and pulled out a wad of cash. He found more in the wallet and put it on the seat. He opened the door and went over to the rail, looking down at the raging river. He took the dealer's clothes, piece by piece, and gave them a toss into the middle of the river. When he'd tossed the last shoe he got back into the truck.

Pulling away Andy pondered, "Ever wonder what happens to these guys we take up there?"

"Nope, don't care either as long as they don't come back." Doug was not the sympathetic type. "So far none of them have, so it must be working."

Andy counted the bills. "There's over a thousand dollars here."

"I don't want any of that drug money. You take it and use it to get your daughter some professional counseling when she gets out of jail."

Andy thought about that. "Using this money to pay for her counseling makes sense to me," as he stuffed the cash into his jacket pocket.

They lived in a small town and nobody wanted drug dealers around. Doug and Andy's method was an efficient way of handling the dilemma. The town's people tried to let the police handle the problem when the dealers started showing up five years ago, but their method was agonizingly slow, inefficient and ineffective.

On top of being a painfully slow process to get them off the streets, once they were finally arrested they were right back on the street selling drugs again in a matter of days. After a year of putting up with it the locals were frustrated and decided to take action. They could not just sit there and watch it infect more of their children and grandchildren.

The café group had an impromptu meeting one afternoon and Doug and Andy said they'd take care of it. Their method proved to be one hundred percent effective, the same dealer never came back. Unfortunately, a new one seemed to show up about every six months. Doug and Andy were getting pretty efficient. The town now had very little drug problems and most of them were at the college. The regulars at the café all knew what was happening. In the unlikely event that someone came around looking for the missing dealer, police or otherwise, nobody would remember anything about him. The system worked and the locals were happy. Some even suspected the police knew what was happening, but were glad to be rid of them. The police were as frustrated as the citizens when their efforts to arrest drug dealers just resulted in them being back on the street within a few days.

Uri complained loudly in his native Russian tongue as he walked down the logging road, naked and alone. The darkness was penetrated by a sliver of moonlight, casting just enough light for him to see where he was going.

"Damn, these rocks are sharp! What am I going to do for clothes, I'm freezing my butt off. If I can find a house maybe somebody will have some clothes out on the line. Or maybe I can get into a barn and find some. If not I'll break into a house and take whatever I need. It must have taken two hours to get up here. I should be near houses soon. I can't take this cold much longer."

Uri was complaining so loudly to himself that it caught Swawa's attention as she walked quietly through the forest, her kittens following stealthily behind her. Stopping to listen enabled her to get a better idea of the sounds origin, then they headed in that general direction. At the edge of the forest, next to the gravel road, they could hear the sound clearly. Her keen night vision told her it was coming from down the road about five hundred yards away. The noise was now familiar, she'd heard this type of noise before and it had her full attention. It had been many months since she'd heard it at Cross Point, but she remembered it distinctly. The jogger had made a tasty meal. She increased her speed and her five kittens kept up the pace. Six cougars hunting together was a formidable hunting party that could take almost any living creature with very little difficulty. For the past month food had been scarce. The six of them could easily eat a deer every day, but their favorite prey had eluded them for over a week and they were plenty hungry. Their last meal three days ago was a skunk, hardly a meal, more of a snack, considering one cougar can eat twenty pounds of meat at a feeding when really hungry.

As they drew closer she saw that it was indeed a two-legged prey. The man stopped suddenly and so did she and the kittens. He didn't turn around, he just stood there in the dark. She was now about forty yards away. Crouching down slightly, she began to move quietly toward him, stalking him. One paw at a time, her footsteps silent. The kittens followed suit in a straight line behind her.

Uri stopped at a fork in the road. "Crap, which way do I go now?" He stood there studying his choices. The road off to the left seemed to be going slightly up hill so he decided to take the road to the right. "Ouch!" he said out loud as the sharp rocks continued to cut into his sensitive feet. The cold added to his misery, feet bloody and painfully cold, it was beginning to deplete his energy.

Swawa and her kittens had pressed themselves tight against the ground, stick still, watching, when the man stopped. They waited, observing, until the man resumed his trek down the road. A hundred feet away Swawa began to follow again, slowly at first, then she broke into a trot and finally to a full run, covering the distance in seconds. She leapt from fifteen feet away and landed squarely on Uri's back with all one hundred forty pounds of fast moving force, knocking him to the ground face down.

"Ah!" he yelled in excruciating pain as she seized his head in her jaws, peeling his scalp off from the forehead to the occipital protuberance in the first two seconds of the attack. Her claws dug into his back and buttocks. "Get off me!"

He twisted quickly and flipped over on his back, giving a swift kick to the cat he knocked her off, but the kittens quickly jumped all over him and Swawa was back on him in seconds. Six cougars all over him, ceasing any appendage available, one seized his groin, slicing into his lower abdomen with razor sharp teeth.

"No, get away from there," yelling as he tried to push it away. She quickly tore out a huge chunk of flesh with surgical precision. Gulping down the whole thing in one swallow she went back for another bite from the lower abdomen.

Swawa lunged at his throat next as he kicked and thrashed about, his arms trying to dislodge the overpowering attackers. Swawa had a good grip on his throat now and was pulling and tearing. All six cats had a firm grip on him, his arms and legs searing with pain, his throat felt like it was on fire as Swawa thrust her head back and forth tearing away a gaping hole in his throat. Blood came gushing out and she began licking it as the warm liquid foamed from the opening. One of the kittens slashed open the chest and stomach cavity with one swift pull from a front paw. The intestines spilled out. The heart and liver are the delicacies and usually the first to be eaten from any prey. Chunks of flesh were torn away as Uri's arms and leg muscles began to jerk around from involuntary spasms.

Photo by Lee Dygert

2

Bull Towns was one of the original Tuskegee airmen. After his honorable discharge from the Army Air Corps he was unable to find a job flying for the airlines. The air travel business was just getting off the ground and there were vacancies, but the Army and Navy were separating an inordinate number of pilots at the end of the war. He had well over the minimum flying hours required, they just did not hire black men to fly for the airlines back in those days. In fact, about the only job a black man could get in the mid-forties was washing dishes, collecting trash, or as a farm hand.

After separating from the Army he had returned to his home state of Washington and had been there for four months looking for a job. He was living with some other black men, who had also been recently discharged from the service. They were all living in a tent at the outskirts of Seattle, looking for work. They shared whatever food they could come up with. A deer hung from a tree near the tent, a result of two of the men chasing it until one was able to get close enough to get a rope around its neck. It provided them with sustenance for weeks.

At the time the roads were made of dirt, usually mud with no sidewalks. It was a dark and rainy day. Twenty yards ahead of Bull was James Simons, president of Simons Timber Company, returning to work after having lunch at a nice restaurant. There were no stop lights, not even a stop sign. Simons walked down the path, preoccupied with thoughts of work, and turned to cross the street without looking.

The oncoming thirty-six Chevy hit him squarely, just before it was struck broadside by a model-T Ford coming from the cross street. The Chevy came to rest with the right rear wheel on top of Simon's chest.

Bull got his nickname because he was a big, muscular man. He'd ran to the scene and assessed the situation. There was another man and two women there by then. Speaking to the other man, "I'll lift up the bumper and you pull him free," instructing the other man.

Simons was barely alive as he lay in the mud next to the car. As an aviator, Bull had been trained in first aid. He applied a tourniquet to a severely bleeding left arm. The other man stopped an oncoming car and convinced the driver to take Simons to the hospital, Bull stayed with him, assuring him that he would be fine in a few days.

Simons was in the hospital for three weeks. The doctors informed him that Bull Towns had saved his life. After another four weeks of recovery at home Simons went back to work. On his first day back to work, walking down the street on the way to lunch, Simons ran into Bull, who was still out looking for work every day. Simons offered him lunch, which drew a lot of attention. It was unheard of for a white man to have lunch with a black man in those days. During that lunch Bull told him of his flying experience. Simons, a deeply religious man, immediately realized that destiny had caused the accident. He had been looking for years to find a faster way to deliver urgently needed supplies to remote logging camps. That fortuitous event began a long relationship between Bull and the Simons Timber Company.

Simons' company bought a surplus army aircraft and Bull flew supplies to remote logging camps, dropping them in via parachute. Occasionally, he ferried logging executives to remote landing strips. Bull saved his income and eventually worked out a deal to buy the airplane. He began teaching people to fly in his spare time and later bought extra small airplanes to rent. He'd taught both of his children the love of flying at an early age, put them through college and now both were airline pilots.

Buck rented an airplane at Arlington field again from his old friend Bull Towns. Buck and Eric walked out to the flight line and went through the pre-flight, checking the engine and external surfaces. When they were satisfied that the airplane was airworthy they got inside and strapped themselves into the seats. Eric read the start engine checklist, item by item. Opening the side window he yelled, "Clear!"

The propeller began to turn and the engine came to life, he checked the fuel flow and engine temperature gauges. Everything checked good so they radioed the tower for taxi instructions, wind and weather outlook for the next two hours. They taxied to the end of the runway and Eric did the before takeoff checklist. Everything looked ready to go, he keyed his mike.

"Arlington tower, this is Cessna 14372, ready for takeoff."

"Cessna 14372, this is Arlington Tower, you're cleared for takeoff, wind is 020 at 10. Have a good flight."

Nervously, Eric turned the throttle up to full speed. After scanning the instruments he took his feet off the brakes and the aircraft began to roll down the runway. When the airspeed indicator hit 60 knots he gently pulled back on the stick and the plane began to climb into the sky. He banked the plane toward the east and headed for the foothills of the northern Cascade Mountains leveling off at 5,500 feet pressure altitude, which was about one thousand feet above ground level. Fifteen minutes into the flight a large flat meadow appeared out in the distance.

They both saw it at the same time, something was streaking across the meadow. With the distance and the altitude it was difficult to tell exactly what it was.

Eric cried out, "Hey look! Is that a cougar chasing a deer?"

"I think you're right, it sure looks like a cougar."

They continued flying toward the meadow, but the two animals had disappeared into the woods by the time they were overhead.

"OK, let's climb to 8,000 feet and do some stall practice next."

"Roger," Eric said and pulled back on the yoke, climbing to 8,000 feet and then leveling off.

"OK, go ahead."

He turned down the throttle and pulled the yoke back. The nose rose until the aircraft began to shudder. He gently pushed the yoke forward and increased the throttle. He practiced stalls for about twenty minutes.

Buck suggested, "Let's turn back to the west and descend to 6,500 feet. We'll do some touch and goes before we land."

Eric turned the airplane to a heading of 270 to leave the mountain range. When the airplane got to

6,500 feet Eric pulled back on the yoke to level off but the stick would not budge.

"The stick won't pull back," he exclaimed.

The plane continued to nose over. Buck grabbed his yoke too and both were pulling back on the yokes, but the airplane continued descending and was now in a steep dive.

"I have the airplane," Buck said gravely, reacting quickly he pushed the yoke forward, causing the airplane to go inverted. They were upside down now and Buck swiftly rolled the airplane over to the upright position. It all happened so fast, upside down then back right-side up, fortunately it didn't last long.

"Wow, that was exciting!" Eric whooped, with a wide grin on his face.

Suddenly the plane began to sputter. Buck intuitively scanned the instruments and saw the fuel flow was decreasing rapidly. The tanks were both nearly full, the temperature at that altitude was slightly below freezing, but the carburetor heat was on and there was no good reason for it to ice up, he could not determine a logical reason for the engine problem. They had pogoed the fuel tanks before they took off and there was no sign of water, so that shouldn't be the problem. However, it couldn't be completely ruled out. He switched the fuel tank to the left feed and then switched it to the right feed and back to cross feed, but there was still no fuel flow. Just then the engine stopped.

Buck pushed the stick forward, putting the nose down slightly as he tried to re-start the engine. The propeller was turning, as it should with no restrictions, but the engine would not even sputter. The airplane was now descending through 3,200 feet, pressure altitude, but they were only about 1,000 feet above ground level. Buck pushed the stick slightly to the left and the plane began a left turn.

"Looks like we may have to make a dead stick landing at that meadow where we saw the cougar chasing the deer a little bit ago. Make sure your seatbelt is tightly fastened and get ready for a rough landing if this thing doesn't restart." The closest manned airfield was Arlington. He tuned in the frequency and keyed the radio.

"Arlington this is Cessna 14372 with an emergency, over." There was no response. They were on a VFR flight plan in a remote area just above the foothills of the northern Cascades and probably out of radio range. He told Eric to keep trying to raise them on the radio.

Buck continued to try to get the engine started, but as he passed 400 feet above ground level he realized it was not going to cooperate.

"Brace yourself Eric, looks like we're going to land here."

The wheels brushed the tops of the evergreen trees as they passed over the edge of the meadow, which was about 1,000 feet long. There was no way for Buck to know how smooth the meadow surface was so he flared the airplane just as the wheels touched the grass and created some aerodynamic braking to reduce their landing roll. At the same time he stomped on the breaks. They came to rest after a short, but bumpy ride.

Eric looked over at Buck with a smile and laughed, "Well isn't this another fine mess you've gotten me into Ollie."

"This would make a fine Laurel and Hardy predicament wouldn't it. Shall we get out and take a look under the hood?"

"Might as well," Eric lamented, "doesn't look like there's going to be any mechanics around here. Are all of the flights going to be this much fun?"

They climbed out of the airplane, unharmed, and looked around at the aircraft, determining that it had also come out, miraculously, unharmed. They opened the engine cover and looked around, finding nothing that looked unusual. Buck went to the rear of the fuselage and opened a hatch. Inside was a small box that was strapped down. Pulling out the box he found a flat screwdriver, a Phillips head screwdriver, a pair of pliers, a spark plug wrench and a mid-sized crescent wrench.

Buck removed one of the spark plugs and held it with a stick next to the engine, to avoid being shocked.

"Crank it over a little," Buck said to Eric. The propeller spun around and it sparked just like it should. Next he took the fuel line going into the carburetor off and fuel came flowing out.

"Look like there's fuel going into the carburetor."

"So what does that mean?" Eric asked. "We're in the middle of nowhere. How are we going to get home?"

"That depends on what's wrong. If we can find the problem, and fix it, we should have enough runway space here in this meadow, if it's not too rough, to take off. If we can't fix it we'll need to come up with another plan, so start thinking."

As he put the line back on the carburetor he had Eric crank the engine again, this time sniffing the air that was being forced out of the spark plug hole as the engine was turning.

"OK, hold it. Doesn't smell like there's any gas getting into the cylinder."

He took a screwdriver and removed the carburetor. There was fuel in the tank and the float seemed to be functioning so he blew in the fuel intake side, but nothing came out of the port.

"Hmm, seems to be plugged up."

He set the carburetor on the white painted trailing edge of the tail flap and checked the position of the jet screw. Unscrewing the jet screw, he carefully counted each turn. The screw needed to be returned to exactly the same position it was in when he put it back. The screw was almost out when the fuel began to flow, revealing a tiny speck of black against the white painted surface of the wing flap.

"Looks like we may have found the culprit," he announced to Eric, as he watched intently. "It probably happened when the airplane went inverted. It's a little like shaking an old jar full of liquid. The sediment becomes dislodged. This airplane isn't really intended for inverted flight and it probably never happened before in its many years of flying."

"You mean that tiny little speck of stuff could have killed us?"

"You could look at it that way."

"Well, how else could you look at it?"

"Flying airplanes isn't for the faint at heart. Our number just wasn't up yet. The more you fly, the more experience you get. The experience helps you to know what to do when you have a serious system failure."

"Well, I'm not worried about it, but it just seems rather innocuous that such a little speck of dirt could cause such a catastrophic failure."

"Things happen when you're flying airplanes. Be flexible and learn to make the best of it. That's why it takes so long to learn how to fly and react instinctively when an emergency happens. If you want to fly airplanes, you need to learn to live with emergencies because they are going to happen, and you never know when. You have to be prepared for it all the time and when it does happen your reactions must be automatic."

Buck put the carburetor back on and told Eric to crank it up. After about twenty seconds the engine caught and fired right up, sounding just like it should. Buck motioned his hand across his throat, giving Eric the cut engines sign.

"Now we'd better check out the flight controls. That diving split 'S' maneuver I had to do to get the flight controls working again had to have been caused by something."

They removed the side panels to expose the mechanical wires that moved the ailerons up and down. Buck studied the wires then reached in and took hold of one, sliding it back and forth. He heard a slight rubbing sound and felt a slight amount of resistance. Sticking his head in a little farther to get a better view he found an old rusty screwdriver lodged between the wires.

Buck announced, "Looks like we found the culprit. That wasn't there when we did the preflight. It must have been left somewhere in the compartment a long time ago. Probably hid itself when a mechanic was working in here and he forgot about it. Eventually it vibrated itself around until it got lodged in the cables here. It's pretty rusty, probably been in there for years. It just decided to cause a problem today."

"Our lucky day," said Eric.

"We had an old saying in the Navy, 'any landing you can walk away from is a good landing'. Let's go have a look around the meadow. Look for big rocks, logs and large holes. Toss the rocks and big branches out of the path."

They started walking around the area, Buck went to the east indicating Eric to go to the west, checking the ground conditions. The wind seemed to be coming from the west and they'd have to take off into the wind, which meant they needed to move the airplane to the other end of the meadow. Preferably soon because they only had about twenty minutes before it would be too dark to attempt a takeoff. They walked the full length of the meadow, checking for holes or anything that could break the landing gear during a takeoff run. Buck threw a few sticks and some bigger rocks to the tree line. It wasn't a runway, but it seemed to be smooth enough to make a takeoff. Satisfied they would be able to make it, he started walking back to the aircraft.

Eric turned around and saw that a wall of black, ominous clouds were rolling in quickly from the east and it was starting to rain. He took off toward the aircraft waving to Buck. The rain was gentle at first, but as the wind picked up, Buck increased his pace. He looked back over his shoulder just as he heard the faint rumble of thunder off in the distance and the wind suddenly began to howl. By the time he reached the airplane lightning was flashing and the sound of thunder rumbled through the previously calm meadow. Eric had beat him to the plane and was holding the side door open for him when he arrived and Buck jumped into the plane. He was wet from the rain, but he made it just in time to keep from being thoroughly soaked. The thunderstorm brought high winds that rapidly changed directions.

"Oh well, so much for making it out of here tonight. Guess we better get on the radio and try to tell Arlington the situation. Since we were on a two hour flight no one will start worrying until we're not back to the airport by the time it gets dark, then they'll start to get worried."

Buck cycled through all the frequencies trying to reach an airfield or flight service station with no luck. Unfortunately, they were in an area where transmission and reception was not good.

"Looks like we'll have to resort to the emergency method. In view of the circumstances I guess we'd better or they'll spend a lot of time and energy trying to find us." Buck switched the radio to the guard frequency 121.5, which was used for emergencies.

"Any station, this is Cessna 14372, on VHF guard, over." After a short pause a reply came.

"Cessna 14372, this is United heavy 1142, go ahead." An airliner traversing the high altitude airways somewhere above them heard the call. All airliners were required to monitor the emergency frequencies 121.5 VHF and 243.0 UHF. Buck figured he'd have no problem getting a message relayed through an airliner under the circumstances. He'd done it for other people many times during his military flying years.

"United heavy 1142 this is Cessna 14372, we're a Cessna aircraft out of Arlington, two people on board, no injuries, we had a fuel blockage and were forced to make a non-airfield landing about 100 miles northeast of Arlington field. We've got the engine running now but will have to wait until morning to attempt a takeoff. Please notify Arlington field we're OK and have Bull Towns notify our family. We'll contact them tomorrow morning after we're airborne or if unable to make a takeoff we'll relay another message for assistance."

"Cessna 14372 this is United heavy 1142, wilco, good luck."

"Thanks for the help, out."

Buck turned to Eric. "We'll wait until morning now to see which way the wind is blowing before we move the aircraft for takeoff. Might as well get comfortable for the night. Good thing we wore ski jackets and warm clothes for the flight, may get cool tonight."

"We could go out and build a shelter for the night after it stops raining. A fire would be nice and it would keep us plenty warm."

"Well, I don't see a good place to make a shelter nearby, it's soaking wet from the storm and it's dark. In here it's dry, well protected, and probably more comfortable than lying on the wet ground. My vote would be for staying in here."

"You've got good points there, guess you're right. A fire would be nice though."

"Probably not a good idea in here," he chuckled, trying to make light of the situation.

Eric was prepared, he put his hand in the jacket pocket and pulled out a handful of heat-producing packets from the inside pocket of the snowboarding jacket he was wearing and handed two over to Buck.

"Here you go." He kept them in the jacket all winter so that they would be handy in the event of a particularly cold snowboarding day.

Buck said, "You're well prepared," Taking off one shoe at a time, he broke open the packet and put it in the toe of his shoe and put the shoe back on.

"Ahh, this is almost as good as a fire."

Each heat-producing packet would keep their feet warm for about 3-6 hours. Eric counted a total of eight packets left, plenty for one night.

Buck found four granola bars in his jacket, giving two to Eric. "I'm not sure how long these have been in my pocket, but I'm pretty sure they're from last ski season. They look good," as he bit into one. "Yep, they're fine."

They discussed the flight and responding to emergencies for a couple of hours, then both dozed off around ten. Shortly after midnight something jarred Buck awake. Looking out the side window of the aircraft he was surprised to see a cougar's face less than three inches from his own, nose up against the plastic window staring right at him. Both front paws were placed on the window, framing the cougar's face. The paws were huge. Buck sat there for a moment looking at it, eye to eye, then slowly nudged

Eric. When he finally came out of his sleep, he looked over at his dad.

"Holy shit!"

Calmly Buck said, "Must be the one we saw chasing the deer across the meadow this morning. He's mostly just curious, but I'd guess he was unsuccessful in his quest to catch the deer."

The cougar bared its fangs, hissing at Buck, claws flexed, its paws pumped at the Plexiglas window. Buck figured it might be time to put a quick end to this development. He reached over and turned the key to the ignition. The engine fired up immediately and the cougar disappeared in the blink of an eye.

The horse whinnied and began to get agitated as forest ranger Rick Dance rode along the mountain trail. Rick pulled back on the reins.

"Whoa there Rusty," as he got the horse under control again. Reaching up he removed the headset he was wearing to track the animal he tagged two weeks ago. Immediately he realized what had spooked Rusty. He looked up toward the sound of a sputtering aircraft engine, directly overhead at a relatively low altitude, just as the engine quit. The airplane immediately began to descend, but the pilot obviously had control because the attitude remained constant. As it continued to descend it went out of sight because of the trees and hills in his field of vision. He didn't hear the engines start up again so if it did go down, it wouldn't be too far away, maybe three to five miles to the east of his position.

Knowing the area well enough, he knew there was an exceptionally flat mesa in the direction the aircraft was headed. The pilot couldn't help but see it. Assuming the pilot would attempt to make a landing there, Rick turned Rusty in the general direction. As he headed off toward the mesa he listened to see if the engines would start up or maybe he'd hear a crash. The mesa was almost all grass and was so flat it looked like it had been graded. Rick had never seen anything like it in his twenty years as a forest ranger. The elk and deer that frequented the area kept the grass mowed down low.

Nearly an hour later a fast moving thunderstorm rolled in. It rained so hard the horse began to slip on the muddy trail. Rick decided he'd better stop before his horse was injured. Riding into the shelter of a stand of trees, he tied the horse up and pulled his tent out of its bag. The tent was a new style dome tent that still amazed Rick. The engineering of the tent allowed it to be fully erected in less than two minutes. All one had to do was pull the nylon string at the top center of the tent and it popped open. After snapping the four bowed stays in place he went inside the lightweight nylon tent that could sleep four people easily. Rick whistled for Goldie, his Labrador retriever, holding the flap open Goldie came quickly and proceeded to shake herself off inside the tent. She could be a nuisance at times, but she was good company when out in the woods for weeks at a time.

Rick, an animal wildlife biologist, had studied cougars for most of his twenty years as a ranger. He had been tracking this particular one for nearly two weeks now. A faint signal could be heard when he put the headset back on. He attached the direction finder and it seemed to indicate that his target was approximately three miles away to the east. Since that was pretty much the direction he was heading to check out the aircraft, it would be right along the way. He did not intend to catch or shoot the cougar; he simply wanted to monitor its behavior and diet. This one was a particularly unusual animal. Over the years he had seen a few similar ones that would kill multiple prey at one time without any intention of eating all of the dead animals. There were a few cases he'd learned of unusual killing sprees. Five years ago a cougar got into a farmer's sheep pen at night and killed all 22 sheep in the pen. Another case was a cougar that attacked a flock of Canadian geese, trying to kill as many as it possibly could before they got away. There were many documented cases of cougars killing far more than they could eat before the meat spoiled. Why this happened was an unknown, but in Rick's experience observing them, it was just sheer instinct to chase and kill anything that was trying to get away.

The rain continued heavy until after dark so he would have to stay there for the night. Rick had spent too many years in the woods to think about traveling after dark, with no moon, slick trails and all. He knew the area well, but the storm could likely have blown down trees over the trail, creating loose rocks the horse would not see in the dark. Plus, in the woods there was always the chance of coming across a bear or cougar and experiencing a surprise attack. The odds were not in his favor for a night ride tonight. When the rain subsided to a fine mist he went outside to the horse pack, pulling out the feed bag he poured some oats into it and put it over Rusty's head, placed some food in a bowl for Goldie and made some dinner for himself. After cleaning up from dinner he decided to retire early so he could be off at first light in the morning.

Bright and early at five a.m., Rick got up and put some coffee on the propane burner. While it perked he put the tent and sleeping bag away and loaded the horse up for the trip. Putting the tent away was almost as easy as setting it up. He hoped whoever invented this magnificent idea was already a millionaire, wishing he'd had one for the last twenty years.

As soon as it was light enough to see, they were on their way. Rick put the headset on to check the location of his tagged cougar. It was still in the general direction he was traveling and about five miles away. At six fifty, Goldie, who was up ahead of him started barking. She'd wandered off the trail so he had to follow the barking sound until he found her next to a dead elk that had been killed less than twenty-four hours ago. Sliding off the horse he examined the carcass, not surprised at what he found. The elk's throat was torn out and the liver had been eaten. That was all, only the liver. He took measurements of the female elk and estimated its age at less than two years, weight about two hundred eighty pounds, and recorded everything in his logbook. If it had been the end of the day, and the kill was a little fresher, he would have sliced off a loin for dinner that night.

About an hour later Rick reached the edge of the meadow, quickly searching around until he saw the aircraft on the far side. Goldie ran ahead to the plane. As he rode toward it he analyzed the aircraft, he could not see any obvious damage and thought it looked to be intact. He pulled out his satellite phone and checked to see what kind of reception he would get. The signal was coming in strong, as he expected, since he was at the top of the mesa and had an unobstructed view for miles in every direction. The phone was only used in case of an emergency. Even though he had a solar charger, battery life was precious out in the woods on his long trips.

Buck and Eric were on the blind side of the aircraft doing a preflight check. They discovered the wheels had sunk into the wet ground overnight. Getting the aircraft to break free would prove to be a challenge.

Goldie came around the plane and gave a single bark.

"Hi there, looks like we've got company," Buck said as he extended the back of his hand toward the dog to see if it was friendly. She moved closer and sniffed at his hand then around his feet, smelling the scent of Buck's dog Scout.

"Seems friendly enough," Eric said as he extended the back of his hand slowly toward the dog. It sniffed and started wagging his tail. Eric ran his hand down the dogs back. "Must be someone with it would be my guess."

When they came around to the other side of the aircraft they saw a man on horseback, riding toward them.

"Howdy," Rick greeted.

"Hi, got a tow truck and a catapult in that saddle bag?" Buck joked.

"Guess if I was Harry Potter I could conjure you up a solution to your predicament and get you on your way. Anybody injured in this incident?"

"Thankfully we're in one piece and so is the aircraft. I think we could actually get it back in the air if we could just get the wheels out of the muddy rut they're in."

Rick got down off of Rusty, extending his hand, he said, "I'm forest ranger Rick Dance, and that's Goldie."

Buck shook his hand, "You know I believe we've met before. We had coffee a few weeks ago at the small café in Arlington with Bull Towns. It's nice to see you again, I'm Buck Logan and this is my son Eric."

"Yes, I remember now. I've been thinking about that meeting. Are you the same Buck Logan that rescued a little five-year old girl who was attacked by a cougar shortly after she got off of the school bus? Seems to me it was about two years ago? As I recall the cougar was dragging the child off into the woods when a guy named Buck Logan killed it with a pitchfork."

"Well yeah, that's me, but how would you know about that?"

"I'm a wildlife biologist. I've been doing research on cougars for years. I read everything that I can find about them."

"That's interesting, we had one come visiting last night. It was around three a.m., looking right into the side window of the aircraft. It had both paws up on the window and its face was about three inches from mine when I woke up, got my full attention right away. It was pretty clear he wanted in, so I started up the engine and he took off like a rocket."

"Must have been your lucky day yesterday. I've been tracking him for fourteen days now and he has killed eleven elk in that time. Odd part is that he only eats the liver, nothing else. For one cougar to kill that many elk in that time span is very odd. This is the most unusual one I have seen in my twenty years of studying them. He's a big one too. Last time I tagged him he weighed 201 pounds. I figure he's about eight years old now. He must be a smart one because they don't get that old in the wild very often. A week ago he killed a coyote and didn't eat any of it."

"In that case, I'm glad we were in the aircraft and not out in a tent for the night."

"Yeah, it was probably a safer place to be, this one is unpredictable. In fact, a lot of them are becoming unpredictable. Before 1990, I had a hard time finding them to do research. They used to be very shy and reclusive. Since the early 90's the cougar population has continued to grow to the point where they are showing up in people's backyards in the city. They're living around people and studying them. I'm afraid they may be trying to learn how to hunt humans. There's so many in western Canada and Oregon they have two or three living in the same roaming area. That behavior is unheard of in cougar history. In fact, a woman was killed while skiing just recently. According to an eyewitness it killed her very quickly because there wasn't even a struggle. A game warden shot it shortly after the attack. It was a four year old male, 138 pounds, and in good health. I've thought for years that if they ever figure out how to attack humans from the rear they will be successful most of the time. People won't even know what hit them.

Understanding the wildlife population is my job and this is one of mother-nature's best tricks. Virtually everyone thinks that the human and cougar interaction problems are being caused by people moving into cougar country. In reality humans have very little, if anything, to do with it. If you look back in history you'll find that there is a deer population cycle. It's about thirty to forty years long. As deer populations steadily rise, the cougar population rises at the same time, because deer are the primary source of food for cougars. When wild animals have a high food supply it stimulates the ovaries to produce more eggs, so the mothers have bigger litters. It's a cyclical overpopulation of cougars that's so consistent that it's almost predictable. Before 1990, a female cougar would have one or two kittens in a litter. In the last five years I see mothers with three to five kittens. Before 1990, a mother would keep her kittens for twelve to twenty-four months before dispersing them. Today they are dispersing them at around eight months. Once the mother disperses them she'll go into heat within a week or two. A female today may have five times as many kittens in her lifetime as she would have ten years ago.

A hungry adult cougar can eat twenty pounds of meat at a time, feeding morning and night when they have a fresh kill. One cougar will usually eat a deer a week, sometimes more when there's plenty around. With the number of cougars we have today they have basically eaten most of the deer in some areas. That's why people occasionally see them in their backyards. They're just following their food source, looking for something to eat.

Today's high cougar population density has caused some to take up a territory in the watersheds inside city limits after they leave their mothers. There is just no other free territory for them to take when the mother dispersed them. They are basically living in people's backyards now without the community knowing it. They're very illusive, and usually hunt in the dark when living in the city, so people just don't see them. Those cougars are living on raccoons, cats, and dogs. They probably won't get as big as one living in traditional cougar territory, but they are still potentially dangerous. It really amazes me that they can live so close to people, sometimes being around people every day, but incidents are still relatively rare. They may become more dangerous if their food supply dries up, since they are living around people all the time. On the other hand, the problem may solve itself. They're cannibals and they may just eat each other up and the problem will go away by itself. I see the remains of cougars that have been eaten by other cougars out in the woods from time to time."

"That's a comforting thought," Buck replied. "It does seem like there are a lot of incidents. We see it in the news about once a month. Last week there was an article about a town in Oregon where they could not let the children at the elementary school out on the playground because there were cougars in the woods next to the playground, growling at the kids."

"I'm afraid it's going to take awhile to solve this puzzle. There's been a big drop in the number of people hunting since 1990 and that probably has something to do with the deer and cougar populations rising so fast. Public opinion is overwhelmingly in favor of the animals, but I just don't understand what people are thinking. They clearly don't understand that a cougar is not a cuddly housecat. These animals are voracious predators and they will kill and eat anything that moves, it's all the same to them. Hopefully it won't take as long to solve your predicament."

"I saw you overhead yesterday as your engine was sputtering and eventually failed. I figured you'd see the mesa here and if you had to do an emergency landing this would be a good place. It was pretty much on my way, so thought I'd check it out."

"We're mighty glad you did," Buck said.

"Maybe old Rusty and I can give you a hand. The plane doesn't look all that heavy." Rick opened his saddlebag and got a rope out.

They tied one end of it to the nose gear and the other to the saddle horn. Buck got behind one wing and Eric behind the other.

"Ready?" Buck asked.

Rick, standing in front of Rusty said, "OK boy, pull," and led the horse forward.

Rusty gave it a good try and the aircraft moved, but it was not enough to get out of the rut. They tried four more times without success. It was close, but the wheels just couldn't quite clear the top of the rut and break free.

Buck said to Rick, "I've got an idea. If I crank up the engine that should give us enough additional power to get it up and out, if it won't spook the horse."

"No problem with ol' Rusty, go for it."

Buck started the engine and Eric got behind the airplane and pushed the tail forward while Rick urged Rusty on. The aircraft pulled right out of the rut and began to lurch forward. Buck applied the brakes while Rick released the rope and quickly got Rusty out of the path of the plane as it came to a quick stop.

"Pretty slick," Rick said when Buck got out of the plane.

"Yeah, now for the big question. Will it make it out of here without help?"

"I've been across this meadow many times. I've never seen anything like it. It's about as smooth as a parking lot," Rick said. "It's really a phenomenon. It may have been leveled off for some reason years ago. Can't imagine why, but the deer and elk sure like it. They keep the grass trimmed about as good as any lawnmower."

"Rick, do you have any toilet paper?"

"That's one of the few things I wouldn't leave home without."

"Could I impose on you for about ten continuous sections?"

"No problem," Rick said as he fished a roll out of his saddlebag.

Buck found a stick about five feet long and tied the ten continuous sheets of toilet paper to one end of the stick and poked the other end into the ground. The wind caused the toilet paper to blow away from the pole. This told Buck which way the wind was blowing and gave him a rough idea of wind speed. The aircraft would need to takeoff into the wind and the greater the wind speed the less speed the aircraft would need to generate to get off the ground.

"That ought to do it. Let's have one last look around at the ground and make sure there aren't any logs, big sticks or rocks in the way that might give us a problem."

Satisfied the ground of the proposed runway area looked good, Buck exchanged addresses with Rick and they all said their 'good-byes'. Buck taxied the plane to the end of the field, turned into the wind, then ran the throttle up to full speed. He watched the toilet paper and when it took a gust of wind he took his feet off the brakes. As they rolled down the grass runway Buck could feel the lift as the aircraft became airborne faster than he had expected. He climbed out to five hundred feet and turned back around flying over the meadow, rocking the wings and waving. Rick stood in the meadow waving back at them and Goldie raced back down the meadow under them, barking.

Buck turned on the radio as he continued to climb out and called Arlington Field. "Arlington this is

Cessna 14372, we're airborne and enroute to your field, ETA twenty minutes, over."

"Cessna 14372, this is Arlington Field, roger, we're all anxious to hear your story."

"OK Eric, it's all yours. Take us home."

Eric took the controls and scanned the instruments. He mulled over the events of the last day. "I'm almost finished with my hunter safety course, that mesa might be a good place to go cougar hunting."

"Why would you want to go cougar hunting?"

"Deer season doesn't open for months."

"I think cougar season is closed now."

"My hunter safety instructor said there's a lot of cougar incidents happening all over the state. That supports what ranger Dance said. The state is keeping the season open all year long this year in hopes of reducing their numbers."

"I'm not that keen on going cougar hunting. We'd better do the approach checklist or we'll have to go around."

Eric completed the check lists and began the approach to the airfield. He looked at the horizontal situation indicator and then the two sets of landing lights on the right side of the landing area. They were all green so he pushed the nose down and landed in the cross hatched area near the end of the runway. After a smooth landing the tower came on the radio.

"Cessna 14372 continue to the delta taxiway."

"Cessna 14372, roger, delta taxiway."

On arrival Bull Towns was standing on the tarmac waiting for them. After they parked the airplane, they all went into Bull's office where he had two cheese burgers, large fries and a coke for each of them, knowing they'd be plenty hungry by the time they got there.

It took them about an hour to tell the whole story. Bull called in Clem, his mechanic, and told him to replace the fuel filter, the carburetor, clean the fuel lines and do a thorough check on all the flight controls. While Bull was telling the mechanic what to do Buck looked around the office and saw pictures of Bull's family everywhere. There were photos of his wife with cats all around her. It looked as if the pictures had been taken in their backyard. She must like cats, there were about twenty of them in each picture.

After Clem left, Buck mentioned the pictures of the woman and all the cats. "Oh, that's my wife, Rose. She loves cats. Whenever one shows up in the backyard she feeds it and it just stays there, joining in with all the others. We're both getting up in years and she's not thinking real clearly some days now. The Doctor says she's got the beginning stages of Alzheimer's disease. The cats make her happy so I can't begrudge her some pleasure."

On the way home Eric asked, "When's my next flying lesson?"

Photo by Lee Dygert

3

Buck woke up before the alarm clock went off. Lying in bed he looked at the ceiling and thought about the events of the upcoming day. The digital face on the clock radio changed over to 6:00 a.m., the time Buck had set it to come on and Bette Midler was singing 'You are my one true friend'. He rolled over and looked at Marie, then gave her a light kiss on the cheek. It was Monday morning and Buck sat up and rolled his feet over the side of the bed less than four seconds after Bette began singing. He slid his feet into the fleece lined leather slippers that his mother had made for him many years ago. They were warm and comfortable, but were really in need of replacement. Some day he thought.

His mother had passed away last year after a four year battle with ovarian cancer. The operations and chemotherapy had taken their toll on her, slowly draining her life away. Buck wasn't sure if it was the cancer that she had finally succumbed to or the chemotherapy. Every time she had chemotherapy she seemed to be worse off than before. She continued to do most of the work around the house and even worked in the garden right up to the last three days of her life. It was obvious to Buck in the last week that she was near the end, but his father was not ready to accept her departure. They had been married for sixty-one years and had rarely spent a night apart until she began to have her operations.

It seemed like something must be going on in their neighborhood. They lived on a cul-de-sac with each property having two to five acres, but there were only five houses. There was cancer in four of the five houses. In one house, the husband had prostate cancer and the wife had pancreatic cancer. Their next door neighbor, Howard, had been diagnosed with liver cancer a year before his mother died. Howard had an operation to remove the diseased part of the liver and seemed perfectly fine afterward. One Friday evening when Buck was visiting his folks Howard came home after his fifth chemotherapy treatment. He was all smiles and said he felt great. The next day he was in the hospital in a coma and died two days later without regaining consciousness.

Buck went down the stairs and turned on the computer, then headed for the coffee maker. As soon as he opened the coffee canister the aroma of the Starbucks wafted through the air to his nose. His eyes lit up as he took a full sniff of the northwest blend. Within minutes he was at the front door slipping on his ski jacket and his Timberland shoes. He hitched Scout, his eight year old female Dalmatian, to the heavy duty retractable leash and headed out to get the morning paper. As soon as they were out the door Scout ran to the full length of the lead, sniffing around to see what new odors had arrived overnight. There was a slight drizzle in the air and it was a brisk forty-two degrees.

By six thirty Buck had delivered a cup of coffee, a banana and the newspaper to Marie, who was still snuggled under the warm covers, trying to open her eyes.

"Good morning honey," as he set the breakfast on the night stand, pulling back the covers he gave her a kiss on the forehead. "It's time to rise and shine."

"Oh no, it can't be time to get up yet," she mumbled.

"I'm afraid so."

Next he checked on each of the children. Wendy was up and yawning trying to figure out what to wear. Eric and Robert were still sound asleep. No small wonder, it was not worth the fight trying to get them to bed at a reasonable ten o'clock. Like his dad had always told him, 'teenagers already know everything there is to know in life. Sometimes you have to pick your battles, they can be counterproductive'.

Back downstairs Buck put the pancake grill on the stove and made a bowl full of batter. Ready for the breakfast gang he pulled up a chair at the computer and checked the stock market, down fifty points at the open, and heading south. Fortunately he had exited the market in January of 2000. It just seemed ripe for a big correction. After studying the worldwide economy until the spring of 2000 he had taken a substantial position in gold mining stocks and then just let them ride.

His twenty years of flying airplanes in the Navy had paid off in terms of retirement. It allowed him to do what he wanted to do, not because he had to. He chose a part-time position teaching an outdoor skills course at the university. His classes were Tuesday, Wednesday and Thursday and his earliest class started at eleven in the morning, giving him plenty of time to get the rest of the family breakfast and on their way.

On Mondays, Wednesdays and Fridays he took a one hour jog, or a brisk walk, sometimes with the dog after the family had all departed. On Tuesdays and Thursdays he would swim two miles at the university recreation center before classes started.

Marie's computer systems management job was also a good income, however the problems in the economy had recently caused a cut back in her work hours to four days a week. This allowed them to play racquetball at the university on Friday afternoons. Many of their neighbors had not fared so well.

The Everhart's, who lived next door, had recently developed a different situation. Sally's parents, in their mid fifty's, had both lost their jobs over two years ago. Neither of them had been able to find new jobs and their house had been repossessed by the bank through foreclosure. Their retirement plans were no help. The company the mother worked for had gone into bankruptcy, but not before the corporate management had used up the entire employee retirement fund in a vain attempt to save the company. The father had an employee directed retirement fund. It had all been in internet and technology stocks and was now virtually worthless. They had become destitute, so Sally offered them a place to live until they found jobs.

The Johnson's, neighbors on the other side of the Logan's, were in their late forties, and both worked for the state. Their divorced daughter had moved in with them about nine months ago. She'd gone to college in California, got married and stayed there. The marriage lasted only four years and produced two children. Some months ago her position with a technology upstart in southern California had been eliminated. Between rent, a big car payment, outrageous medical insurance premiums, and over ten thousand dollars of credit card debt she was in financial trouble immediately. Her ex-husband was also unemployed and she had not received child support payments for months before her job was eliminated.

Nearly a year after she lost her job the unemployment payments stopped and she still had not found a job. She was evicted from her apartment and her car was repossessed the same week. She had nowhere else to turn so she and her children moved in with her parents. She searched for work all day every day in the local area since she had arrived, but had no luck finding a position in the northwest either. Frustrated, the parents had recently paid for a trip for her to go back to California, visit friends and try to find a job there. She came back after two months with no job prospects, but it was soon discovered that she now was pregnant.

Wendy came down the stairs, all smiles. "Good morning Dad. What's for breakfast?"

"Would you like pancakes or waffles?"

"Oh, a waffle sounds great, with peanut butter and grandma's special raspberry jam."

"You're in luck, the waffle iron is already hot," as he spooned the mix onto the waffle maker. "Better savor every bite of grandma's jam, it's the last jar we have left of her special recipe."

Eric and Bob said "Good morning Dad," wide awake after their showers and both took a chair at the table. The pancakes were ready and Buck laid four on each plate. Bob took the apple juice out of the refrigerator and poured a glass. Eric chose milk, squeezed a generous helping of honey onto his pancakes, then layered a coating of oat bran on the top of them.

Marie walked into the kitchen wearing a beige skirt and matching blazer with a mint green silk blouse underneath, "Morning honey," wrapping both arms around his shoulders and gave Buck a kiss square on the lips.

Hanging in the embrace a little too long Eric said, "Get a room."

Laughing, Marie poured a fresh cup of coffee. Buck announced, "You're on your own tonight. I'm going out to Dad's to help him pull out the old apple tree in the back yard. I expect it'll be a long job and I'll most likely stay there for dinner."

Marie said, "No problem, I may be a little late this evening so I'll bring home a couple of pizza's."

"Make sure it's Papa Murphy's. I want chicken garlic," said Wendy.

Eric and Bob both said, "Make mine pepperoni."

By seven thirty they were all out the door and Buck went to the bedroom to change. He would forego the usual morning walk today since he'd get plenty of exercise removing the tree. Once he had his denim pants on he slid the cell phone into the side leg pocket, made especially for that purpose. He chose a long sleeve blue hunting style shirt with pockets on the sleeve and small specialty pockets on top of the regular flapped breast pockets. Downstairs Buck picked up the TV remote and turned off CNBC, then the computer. At the back door there was a six foot long, three level shoe shelf holding a variety of shoes in a mix of sizes and styles. He chose a pair of high top nylon mesh hiking shoes. While he was in the Navy they'd spent over ten years living in the islands where it was customary to leave shoes at the door. The practice was handy in the northwest also because of the constant rain and mud.

Buck opened the door into the garage and said "Let's go Scout. It's time to go see Dad."

Scout ran to the car with her tail wagging hard enough to knock over almost anything it hit. Buck pressed the garage door opener on the wall as he came through the door and the big double garage door began its noisy climb up the wall. As soon as he opened the back door of the forest green SUV, Scout jumped in. Quickly making her way to the front seat, she looked out the side window in anticipation of the ride to come. When Buck climbed into the driver's seat he looked over at her.

"Oh no you don't, you know better than that," hiking his thumb toward the rear. Scout, tail between her legs, reluctantly returned to the back where the seats had been folded down. Buck pressed the rear window button and lower the window about eight inches so Scout could stick her head out into the wind stream.

There was a hint of blue sky in the distance and a gentle breeze against the solid green on each side of the road as he pulled onto I-90. The fir, hemlock, cedar, alder, maple and spruce ascended from the edge of the road up the side of the mountain in a solid, undulating wall. The drizzle stopped as he reached the peak of the cascades and started down the east side of the mountain on the forty minute ride to his childhood home. He was glad the weather was improving, though a little rain never stopped people in the northwest from doing whatever needed to be done. The rain may slow down the project some, but if you wait for a dry day on the west side of the Cascades you're in for a long wait.

Where Buck lived the annual rainfall was about fifty inches. Thirty-five miles east, where he grew up, the annual precipitation was twelve inches, much of which was snow. The eastern summers were dry and hot. The difference in the amount of rainfall was apparent immediately. When he started down the eastern side of the mountains the green wall of trees slowly changed to more open spaces. Smaller trees that were spaced farther apart and bushes that were smaller and more adapted to a dryer climate. The more arid type of terrain was in sharp contrast to the surroundings only ten minutes before.

Buck exited I-90 at the Easton off ramp and turned into Jack's driveway within ten minutes. Scout, with her face up against the back window, recognized the scenery and began wagging her tail vigorously. It was a well established neighborhood with each house on two acres or more of land. The back of each property was woods and open spaces. The house was located at the outskirts of the small town, but it was only a five minute drive to the center of town.

The area had been a major logging industry before the environmental movement shut it all down. Buck's father had been one of the many unfortunate casualties. Since he was over sixty-five when it happened he was able to collect Social Security. He wasn't ready to retire at the time and probably could have worked for another ten years, but that wasn't one of the choices.

Today the town was held together by accommodating the Seattle tourists, campers, fly-fishermen, snow-mobiles and the few city hunters that steadfastly held on to their sport. Many of the locals were serious hunters and kept meat on the table by subsistence hunting. It was not a prosperous town, but everyone who lived there loved it. For those hearty, independent mountain folk, a move to Seattle to find work would be a fate worse than death.

Seeing Buck's dad standing just inside the garage Scout quickly jumped to the front seat when Buck pulled into the driveway. Buck stepped out of the car and Scout shot out behind him heading straight for Jack.

"Hello Scout," he said as he bent over and rubbed the back of her head with both hands.

Buck and Jack hugged, "Hi Dad, how are you doing?"

"Well I'm still alive and kicking. Are you ready to take out that old apple tree?"

"Not really, I used to sit under that tree in the heat of summer eating a fresh apple, just enjoying the quiet serenity. Too bad it has to come out."

"Well, it's dead. Not much sense leaving it there. We can cut it up for fire wood."

Jack was eighty-three now, but he could still handle a chain saw. One pull and it fired right up. First he trimmed off the major branches that he could reach from the ground. Then he stepped back and took a good look at the tree. The saw hung at his side chugging away as he calculated where he wanted it to fall. He walked back and cut a small wedge out of one side about three feet off the ground, then sawed through the trunk at an angle from the other side. The tree landed exactly where he knew it would.

"OK, I'll take it from here." Buck took the saw from his dad and began trimming off the remaining branches. He sectioned off the trunk into fireplace sized logs, using the side length of the chain saw blade as a measuring tool. Next, he cut up the branches using the same method. Now came the least fun part of the project, the stump removal. Buck backed the SUV up to the stump and they laid two wraps of chain around the base of the tree, attaching the other end to the trailer hitch. Buck got in and put it in four wheel drive, slowly tightening the chain.

After letting off and giving it another try a few times it hadn't budged.

Jack said, "Hold it, the dang thing isn't going anywhere."

Buck got out to check the lack of progress.

"I know how to solve this puzzle." He went to the back of the garage and attached a high pressure nozzle to the hose. Turning on the water to full blast, he began excavating the dirt from around the base of the tree, shoving the nozzle deep down into the root system every three to four inches at the base of the tree.

"What are you doing? You're making a mess."

"Well, we're never going to get it out by just pulling on it. If we have to dig it out, we'll be at it for days. You want the tree out?"

"Yes, it's time for it to go."

"Watch, this will serve a dual purpose."

Jack scratched his head wondering what Buck was up to.

After using the hose for about fifteen minutes the whole area was muddy, but thoroughly saturated.

"OK, let's give it another try," as Buck rinsed off his shoes and crawled into the SUV.

This time the tree came right out of the ground on the first pull. Buck got out of the SUV and took a look at the stump and then at Jack.

"Well I'll be," Jack intoned. "Guess you just have to be smarter than the tree."

Around four in the afternoon they stacked the last of the apple tree on the wood pile.

"Apple wood is really good burning wood. This stack should last most of next winter if I blend it in with some fir. I'm sure going to miss those apples though," Jack said.

Buck went over to the back of the SUV and withdrew a four foot high apple tree start.

"I thought you might feel that way. You know the old Boy Scout motto, 'be prepared'."

The hole was already open for them, in fact it was way too big so Buck shoveled some soil back into the hole. The soil was sandy and the water had drained relatively quickly. Jack held the tree in place while Buck filled the dirt in around the roots of the new tree.

"I say that's about enough for one day," said Jack. "How about a beer?"

"I am a bit hot and sweaty, a beer sounds good."

They dusted themselves off and headed for the house. Scout had been out in the woods running around, chasing anything she could find. When she saw them walking toward the house she beat them to the door.

In the kitchen Jack took out a handful of dog biscuits and gave her one, pocketing the rest for later. At the refrigerator he pulled out two bottles of Hefferwisen and handed one to Buck.

"Let's go sit on the porch. It's still nice enough outside." He extracted two Cuban cigars from the humidor on the mantle and they moved to the porch, each one settling in their favorite chairs. It was illegal to sell Cuban cigars, or anything else Cuban in the U.S., but not in Canada, and Canada was not that far away. Buck took the offered cigar and slowly lit it, taking in the sweet, mild, aroma. The only time he smoked cigars was when he was with his dad and it was usually some kind of special occasion.   He figured this was a special occasion. That apple tree had been there for a long time, even before he was born.

It was a sort of boyhood monument and he had a sentimental attachment to it. His first real kiss was under the branches of that old apple tree. Gail, the girl next door, was over watching a movie one night. When it was over he walked her home, but they ended up sitting under the tree. It was a hot summer night, the stars were shining and the Milky Way was an omnipresent sight. They were both fifteen at the time and he still remembered the oneness that they felt and wondered what she was doing today. Her family had moved away to the west side of the Cascades during the winter of that year. Funny, how those things that seemed so important in high school, had faded into the morass of time. Insignificant thirty years later as time marched on, but still, an unforgettable evening in a chapter of his life.

"We haven't had much chance to talk, chain saw makes a lot of noise," Buck said.

"That it does. How are the kids?"

"The kids are doing fine. Eric completed the hunter safety course and got his hunting license. The neighborhood's changed a bit though. Sally Everheart's parents just moved in with them. Both lost their jobs some time ago and couldn't find new ones. They even applied at all the fast food restaurants. At their age, in this economy, they may never work again. Johnson's, on the other side of us, had their daughter and two kids move in with them some months ago."

"It's all part of the cycle," Jack commented. "We're going into a depression. It happens every fifty to sixty years, just like clockwork. Read Robert Prichter's book, _AT THE CREST OF THE TIDAL WAVE_. It's full of statistics, but it makes a pretty good case about depressions being cyclical. I think depressions are caused by the invention of some new technology that changes the homeostasis of society in a dramatic way. The last depression was caused by the invention of the automobile and eventually, the assembly line. It transformed a horse drawn farm society into one that forged the new frontiers of automobiles and gasoline. It made Henry Ford, J. Paul Getty, and the Rockfeller's the wealthiest people in the world. The problem was nobody knew how to do the maintenance on cars, gas stations, tires, roads and everything else associated with the auto. It was all new. It took time for people to learn the new jobs that go with the new technology. Can you imagine what life would be like today without the automobile?

This depression will be caused by the invention of the computer and the follow on expansion of the internet. The computer, the software that determines what computers can do, and the internet have changed everything, just like the automobile and the assembly line did. Very few people today know how a computer works, much less how to program or maintain one. In ten years from now a computer will be as simple to use as an automobile is today and every one will know how to use it. Anything that isn't as simple to operate as a telephone won't survive. In the mean time, those who have developed this new technology will get rich. The workers in this field will soon see their inflated salaries come back to reality as the depression progresses.

The scary part is the unknown. What is going to happen in the meantime while things move back to homeostasis? The rest of the world is in much worse shape than the U.S. right now. If other countries continue to devalue their currency, eventually the U.S. will have to follow suit in order to export and stay competitive in the world market. It isn't just the United States, it's a world wide phenomena. I was in my early teens when the last depression was in full swing. My parents lost their farm, so did your mother's parents. Nobody could make the payments on their land. We actually lived out of our car for awhile before we lived in a tent city on the outskirts of what was left of the town. That's where I met your mother. She was living there in the tent city too. Her father had planted fifty acres of cantaloupes that season, not knowing that the banks were going to close. People went to the banks and started withdrawing cash, but the banks didn't have enough cash. The federal government couldn't print enough money to cover the deposits in such a short time and there was no way the federal government could back all the deposits. By the time the crops were ready to pick the banks had re-opened, but the dollar had been devalued and no one could afford to buy cantaloupes. They were a luxury item then. The whole field had to be plowed under, stunk to high heaven. My dad had peach tree orchards, couldn't sell peaches either. Our homes and farms were repossessed by the bank.

I'm glad I'm on social security this time. The government is always the last to feel the pinch of economic contraction. It all takes time, but as the unemployment rate increases the government receives less in tax revenue. If it goes on long enough the government finally gets into trouble. It may happen faster this time. Governments across the country have been spending like a drunken sailor on shore leave.

Today, with revenue way down from what it was in the prime of the computer and internet expansion, the city, state and federal governments haven't even considered cutting back on capital expenditure. That's what's really going to get them."

"How do you think this'll effect my retirement check?"

"Don't know, I was too young when it happened before to remember much about the mechanics of how it worked. That's part of the problem. With a fifty to sixty year cycle, the corporate memory is gone. So nobody sees it coming or knows what to do when it gets here."

"Maybe we'll end up doing some hunting again like we used to. Eric's chomping at the bit to go hunting now that he has his license. Seems to think he's going to go cougar hunting. Hardly sounds very appetizing though."

"I've heard they are good eating, but I can't remember ever having any. Every once in a while someone around here gets one. It's usually by accident though, when their cat or dog is being eaten by one in their backyard.

Around here people don't think much about shooting a predator that's eating one of their animals. I've heard people who live just outside the suburban growth area will sit and watch a cougar eat their dog on their front porch and feel guilty about moving out of the city. Kind of makes you wonder if they'll accept that same animal eating one of their children in their backyard. City people don't have to deal with the same problems that we, out in the country, live with every day, so they don't think the way we do. The bottom line is that you can't have city people making rules for people that live out in the country."

"Having lived on both sides of the equation that makes sense to me, but most city people have never lived in the country," Buck said. "They don't understand the reality of the things that country people live with everyday. A city person would not tolerate a cougar in their backyard with their children for a nanosecond. They'd have half the city's public safety department in their backyard in a matter of minutes. But if it's someone out in the country they say, 'that's what you get for living out there'. Regardless of whether it's in the city or the country, it's still a public safety issue."

"If Eric is hell bent to go cougar hunting, don't let him go alone," Jack replied.

Photo by Lee Dygert

4

Eric cruised into the mall parking lot in his Ford Ranger pick-up truck and found a spot close to the food court entrance. It was a little after seven p.m. on a dark, rainy, northwest Saturday evening. He'd called his pal Jeremiah after he got off work from his lifeguard job at the city pool and they'd made a plan to meet at the mall. There was a bit of a breeze so Eric flipped up the hood on his Central Washington University sweatshirt to ward off the cold. When he walked into the mall he saw Jeremiah right away, sitting at a table drinking a latte.

"Hey dude, what's up?"

"I thought you were going to call me on your cell phone and find out where I was when you got here so we'd meet up."

"Didn't need to, I saw you as soon as I walked into the mall. But, if it'll make you feel more important I'll call ya now."

"Naw, no sense in it now."

"Shall we take a hike around the mall and see if there's any good looking chicks to strike up a conversation with?"

"That's why we're here," Jeremiah responded.

They walked around the mall, making three complete trips end to end, wandering through the stores, especially the hip clothing stores where teenagers were most likely to be checking out the wares; Gap, Millers Outpost, American Eagle, Zumie's. The mall was pretty much empty except for the sales clerks in the stores, most of whom were slightly older than them. It was a miserable night to be out, but it was typical northwest spring weather. People were accustomed to being out when it was cold and rainy.

As they passed the food court Jeremiah got a whiff of the teriyaki chicken. "Time for some food, I'm starving."

"You're always starving. You eat more than anybody I know."

"I'm a growing boy. I've got six feet four inches to keep full of food."

"I could use something to eat myself. I haven't had anything to eat since I went to work at two. That rice bowl looks good," as Eric eyed the Kung Pow chicken. "I'll take a couple of spring rolls too," he said to the man behind the counter.

"You sure lucked out when you got that lifeguard job," Jeremiah said when they sat down to eat.

"Yeah, where else can you get paid to sit around and watch girls in their bathing suits? A lot of the people that use the pool tend to be in their fifties and sixties, but there's a swim club that uses the pool after school for a couple of hours. There are some nice looking girls on the team. This summer I'll be guarding at the lake, and there is plenty of chicks around there. I have to admit, it sure beats working in a fast food place."

After putting down a few more bites Eric asked, "How long have you been hunting?"

"About six years, no, this was my seventh season deer hunting. Started hunting with my dad when I was twelve."

"Ever see any cougars?"

"I've seen at least one each year for the last three years. Never saw one before that."

"I finished the hunter safety course last weekend and I got my license yesterday. The instructor said they are keeping the cougar season open all year this year because there are so many of them. I'm thinking about going cougar hunting."

"Bad idea."

"You want to go with me?"

"No way."

"Why not?"

"Two years ago my dad and I were deer hunting up in the Castle Rock area. We were watching a meadow where we usually get a deer each year. Just as the sun was coming up we saw a nice big buck come out of the woods. It was moving real slow, just chewing at the grass. I took a bead on it and then all of a sudden it took off like a bolt of lightning. My dad touched my shoulder and said 'look'. As I let the rifle down I saw a cougar running across the meadow after the deer. Only took it a hundred yards or so to catch up and it jumped in the air about twenty feet away, landing right on its back. Knocked it to the ground, had its claws dug into the back of the deer and was chomping down on the back of its neck. Took one paw and reached around the head and gave a pull. Broke its neck, just like that. The deer never even twitched a muscle, like it was dead instantly. Two hundred pounds of deer, and down in a matter of seconds. I consider myself lucky to have seen it. Most hunters spend years hunting and never see anything like it, pretty awesome. Those things are pure muscle, teeth and claws.

"So why didn't you shoot the cougar?"

"What for? Cougar meat doesn't sound very appetizing to me."

"I suppose you've got a point there. Rick Dance says that there are a lot of them right now. He's the ranger that helped us get the airplane out of the mud so we could take off when we made that emergency landing on the mesa. He does cougar research. He says there's so many of them, they're having to move in closer to the human population. That's why they're showing up in people's backyards."

"Well, they don't belong in backyards, that's for sure. What I saw happened out in the woods, where they're supposed to be. Why shoot it if I'm not going to eat it?"

"Dad killed a cougar, I want to get one too."

"That was different. Your dad killed that cougar because it was about to eat Sally May. Besides, it was a little one. It only weighed about sixty or seventy pounds. The one I watched kill the deer weighed about two hundred pounds. I've heard from other hunters at deer camp that they don't like being shot either. It's a cat, they have nine lives. A few years ago when dad, grandpa and I were hunting up at Table Mountain we were sitting around the campfire with a few other hunters one night and an old guy who'd been hunting for about sixty years said cougars can get up and attack a hunter after they've been shot two or three times. After watching that cougar take down the deer I don't think I'm too keen on having an up close and personal experience with one."

Sally Everhart, Buck's next-door neighbor, drove up her driveway after delivering her children to school.

They had missed the bus again today. It was the third time they'd missed the bus this week. As she got out of the car Buck was walking up his driveway with the morning paper.

"Morning Buck, did you read in the paper this morning about the cougar hunter that was attacked by a cougar he'd already shot?"

A little over a year ago Buck saved the life of her daughter, Sally May. She'd just gotten off the school bus when a cougar dropped out of a tree from above the bus and dragged her off into the woods. A neighbor who was across the street waiting for her children, saw it happen and began yelling that a cougar had grabbed Sally May and dragged her off into the woods. Buck had been out working in the yard, grabbed a pitchfork out of his garage and ran into the woods after them. Following the trail for about ten minutes he came across the cougar and Sally May. He was able to frighten the cougar off and pick up Sally May, but as he was carrying her back to safety the cougar attacked them. Reacting to the attack with quick thinking, he skewered it with the pitchfork in a heated, but short fight.

"No, I haven't had a chance to look at the paper yet. Everyone was running late this morning and I'm just now picking it up."

"Apparently, the hunter shot the cougar right through the heart, but it attacked him anyway."

"Killed him?"

"Yeah, another hunter found him later in the day, and the cougar was lying dead on the ground about 100 yards away. The paper said that the cougar was eight years old and weighed 181 pounds. It had been shot once, right through the heart. I think the article said with some kind of big hunting rifle, a 30.06 sounds right."

"Wow, that's pretty scary. Doesn't sound like cougar hunting alone is such a good idea, even with such a big gun, a 30.06 is a very powerful rifle."

Sally had been an avid environmentalist and animal rights activist for many years, but that was before her daughter was attacked by a cougar, right in front of their house. They lived in a nice development of a suburb at the foothills of the heavily wooded Cascade Mountains. What was a cougar doing around all these people? When it happened she was afraid she would never see her daughter alive again. Then when Buck came out of the woods carrying her daughter alive, she'd ran to them crying. Her prayers had been answered and she would be forever grateful to Buck for saving her daughter.

Today, she was still very much the environmentalist, but no longer an animal rights activist. Cougar articles appeared in the paper and on TV from time to time. She wondered why this was happening, thinking they were such beautiful animals, but they just don't belong in town around people. The cougar incidents had started appearing on the nightly TV news and in the paper about three years before, and increased in frequency since then. It seemed now that hardly a month went by without hearing about another incident somewhere.

Sally was beginning to wonder about the animal rights movement. Some of these people were really fanatical. She could clearly remember the last meeting she attended at Forevergreen University, a month before Sally May was attacked. One man had stood up in the meeting to speak and said we need to get rid of some of the people! Incredibly, a number of others had agreed. Sally thought to herself, you condone killing people, but not animals! After that, she had been less enthusiastic about the movement, but when Sally May was dragged off into the bushes to be eaten by a cougar, that event changed her life forever.

Last week her elderly aunt had mailed her a newspaper clipping from the town where she lived, Redlands, California. A densely populated town about fifty miles east of Los Angeles, nestled at the foothills of an arid mountain range. Apparently, a five year old boy got up at six in the morning, walked down the hall, through the kitchen, and into his parent's bedroom where he crawled into bed with them. Shortly after, a mountain lion crashed through the closed kitchen window. It had watched the boy walk through the kitchen and it was just going in after breakfast. When the parents heard the crash they closed the door and called 9-1-1 thinking a burglar had broken into the house. The mountain lion ran around inside the house, went into a bedroom, where a three year old was sleeping, and jumped through another closed window. A man, out for an early walk, heard the noise and looked over to see the mountain lion running straight at him. Ten feet away it veered off and ran up the street.

When the man was interviewed on the TV news that night he said, "It was a big one."

When Eric arrived home from school he declared, "I'm going cougar hunting."

"Maybe you ought to read the article in the paper today first," as Buck handed him the paper. Eric took the paper and read about the hunting incident.

"After reading the article, I'd say cougar hunting doesn't sound like a very good idea," Buck reflected.

Defensively, Eric responded with, "I'm 18, I've got my hunting license, and I can go hunting if I want to."

"What are you going to use for a gun?"

"Your 30.06."

"What if I say no?"

"Then, I'll borrow Jeremiah's."

"Isn't Jeremiah going with you?"

"No, he doesn't have any interest in cougar hunting. Says it could be dangerous."

"Jeremiah's been hunting for years, maybe he's right. Did you read the article?"

"Yeah, but the guy was just unlucky. He probably didn't know what he was doing."

"About as unlucky as you can get. So, you're saying that you do know what you're doing? How many times have you been cougar hunting?"

"Well, I'd do a lot of studying first so I would know what I'm doing."

"Great! I can hardly wait until Mom finds out about this revelation."

That night at the dinner table Marie couldn't believe what she was hearing. "You know, I always thought by the time you were eighteen you'd have learned many things, mainly making good choices. I figured you'd have more common sense than to think about doing something down right stupid, like cougar hunting. It's as simple as this, you're not going!"

"Mom, I'm 18 and I am going! Dad killed a cougar with a pitchfork, it can't be that dangerous."

"Dad didn't go out cougar hunting. It was an unplanned event that happened by accident. He wasn't hunting he was just trying to save Sally May. When it attacked him it was a self preservation reaction. Besides, it was a fairly young one. Cougar hunting is dangerous."

"The cat in the article was 181 pounds. That's a fair sized cat," Buck added to the conversation.

"Well, maybe I'll pick one a little smaller."

"I don't think you really get a choice. Cougar hunting is not that easy. You take what you find, and

I hear they're hard to find without dogs. It's quite possible that you'd end up being the one stalked by the cougar."

"I'll take Scout with me."

Buck could only shake his head, "Scout wouldn't know a lion if it bit her in the butt. Besides, I think it's illegal to have a dog with you when you're cougar hunting, even if it isn't trained."

That night in bed Marie asked in alarm, "We can't let him go. How are we going to stop him from going cougar hunting?"

Buck tried to reassure Marie, "We'll think of something. Now that he's finished the hunter safety class, he's ready to go out hunting. Deer season is closed until next fall. Maybe cougar is the only thing open now. Hopefully it'll just blow over. Let's give it a little time. We'll just try not to bring it up again. The more he talks about it, the more he'll want to go."

"I don't know. He seemed pretty determined."

"Well, it's a sure thing he can't go alone."

Horrified Marie asked, "You mean you'd go with him? Neither one of you should be going."

"I have no interest in cougar hunting at all, but I'm certainly not going to let him go alone."

"That's just great. I can't believe you're even considering it." Marie laid there, eyes wide open and staring at the ceiling.

Rolling over Buck turned the bedside lamp on, picked up the newspaper and began reading the article again.

Bill Wilson lived in a small town in the Cascade Mountains. The town's Main Street was barely a mile long, with two streets of houses on either side of Main Street, deep in the heart of cougar country. Bill was 42 years old and had been hunting for over 30 years. His father, a well-seasoned woodsman, took him out on his first deer hunt when he was ten years old. He'd tagged at least one deer or elk every year since then. In his small town, hunting was not only good sport and recreation, for some it was subsistence. Many incomes in the small town were on the low end of the economic spectrum.

This winter his town had been experiencing a problem with cougars coming into town, taking cats and dogs. Recently, there had been cougar sightings on a regular basis in the early evening, prowling through people's yards. When the fish and game department was called in, the agency responsible for management of large predatory animals, the officer told the resident that it was more a stray cats and dogs problem. He had been called out numerous times that winter, but he steadfastly refused to do anything about it so the town called a meeting.

When Bill arrived at the meeting, he was surprised at the number of townspeople that were present. There was over one hundred in attendance. Considering the small size of the town the problem was getting a lot of attention.

His neighbor got up during the meeting and said, "I've lived here for seventy years and I've never heard of a cougar in town till this winter. Last night I went out to the woodshed to get some wood around nine o'clock. When I came out, there was a big cougar crouched there waiting for me. I dumped the whole armload of wood right at it, got back into the shed, closed the door, and started yelling until my husband came out to see what was going on. By then, it was nowhere to be seen."

Margaret, another of Bill's neighbors, got up and said, "I was on my way to work at the grocery store at five a.m. this morning and there was a huge cougar laying in the middle of the street at the school bus stop, right at the elementary school. It wouldn't move, even after I pulled right up next to it and honked the horn. I had to drive around it. This is about the fifth time the same thing has happened in the last two months. This whole situation is ridiculous. We shouldn't have to live like this. I've got grandchildren playing in my yard. I want that thing out of here."

The mayor got up and asked the fish and game officer, "Why is this happening? It's never happened before."

The fish and game officer got up and said, "I haven't seen any deer or elk in the area for over three months. That's pretty unusual. There is also a very high cougar population in the area this year. They may have consumed all of their normal food supply. "

"So, now they're in town eating our cats and dogs?"

"It hasn't hurt anyone," came the lame reply.

"Are you nuts?" Margaret replied.

"Cougar attacks on humans are very rare and you are living in cougar country. As long as it isn't bothering anyone it is illegal to harm it, unless you have a big game hunting license with a cougar tag and its cougar season. However, keep in mind that it's illegal to discharge a firearm within the city limits."

The sheriff stood up, "I say shoot it on sight."

The officer announced, "If anyone shoots it I'll have to arrest them."

The town mayor said, "This is preposterous. We have an animal that is easily capable of killing any one of us, in town regularly, and we can't do anything about it?"

The warden replied, "In the last fifteen years, there has been an average of one person killed per year by a cougar in all of North America. There's more people killed by automobiles in this state alone every day."

The sheriff said, "I'm the law here and I'm responsible for public safety. In my opinion, this is a public safety issue and I say shoot it on sight or call me and I'll shoot it."

The warden answered, "If you do, I'll be required to arrest you."

"I'm the law here, you can't arrest me."

"I'm also a commissioned officer of the law but I'm commissioned by the state and my commission is superior to yours."

The mayor asked the warden, "Why don't you just tranquilize it and take it up into the mountains, where it belongs?"

"There's two reasons; one, every time we do anything to a cougar the animal rights activists, that live in downtown Seattle, are beating on the doors of the capital the next day yelling animal cruelty. The second reason is, it has been tried before, many times, and we've found they are a lot like house cats in some ways. If I take it a hundred miles away into the woods, it will find its way back here."

Margaret says, "Next time I see that damned thing in the road I'm going to run over it."

The warden replied, "There are quite a few cougars killed by cars every year. That's usually considered an accidental death."

The wheels in Margaret's head started clicking. She could hardly wait for her early trip to work tomorrow morning.

The mayor got up, "This is crazy. I'm with you, sheriff. If you have to shoot it I'll go with you to the capital and set these idiots straight. In the mean time, I'm going to contact our state representative and find out all the legalities behind this mess. Someone up there has to have at least a little common sense."

When the meeting was over some of the frustrated town people were ready to run over the warden. Let him be part of the statistics, but he's only the messenger. It's the people living in big cities like Seattle, New York City and L.A. making up the rules, people who've never been in the woods, much less had to live with the downside of the rules they make up.

When Bill got home he let the dog out for its evening walk around the house. Shortly after the dog walked off the porch a cougar came out of the shadows and pounced on the dog, grabbing it behind the neck. Bill watched it happen and he yelled and screamed, waving his arms above his head. The cat paid no attention to him. Bill ran into the house to get his gun, but by the time he got back the cougar had disappeared with his dog. Bill hunted around the neighborhood for over an hour, but he couldn't find it. He remembered what the warden had said, 'this is life in the woods and he couldn't do anything about it'. Bill decided to solve the problem his own way. Shoot, shovel and shut up.

Early the next morning Bill headed out. It was early spring and there was a light snow on the ground as he started the hunt, alone. This was nothing new or unusual for him, he'd hunted alone for years and was comfortable with it, but usually he took his dog along for company. He started directly behind his house, up a hill to the north of the center of town and found the tracks in the snow within thirty minutes.

He could see clearly where it had dragged his dog in the snow. The trail led him deeper into the woods. About three hours later he found the remains of his dog, completely consumed. The paw prints indicated this cougar was a big one. In his mind he could recall from the fleeting glimpse he had the night before, indeed, it was a big one. The sight of his dog's remains made him even more determined to track it down and kill it. A cougar wandering around town was much too dangerous, especially in the dark. People were right on top of it before they even saw it. If it keeps coming into town it's bound to kill someone.

As the sun dropped lower on the horizon, he knew he had to turn back. The next day he drove his pickup and camper as close as possible to the place where he ended the hunt last night. Picking up the track, he continued the hunt all day again, returning to the pickup at dark. Driving again, to get up as close to the place where he'd stopped, he made some dinner and went to bed. The next morning he got up early, made breakfast and coffee, took a thermos, and resumed the hunt at daybreak. He repeated this process for four days.

On the fifth day he found a freshly eaten skunk, and there was still fresh blood on the snow. It wouldn't be long now, he thought. It had snowed lightly last night and the tracks were very new. He followed them for about an hour, when suddenly, the tracks looked deeper and fresher. Raising his rifle to his shoulder, he felt it was close now. Clicking the safety off, he concentrated on the tracks as he followed. Then abruptly the tracks stopped.

He thought, "What the hell?"

Slowly his gaze moved up the trail and forward to the base of a big cedar tree about fifteen feet away. Running his field of vision up the trunk of the tree, there, about twenty feet off the ground, was a huge cougar. It was crouched on a relatively small branch for the size of the cougar, looking right at him with a fierce look in its eyes, ears pinned back, fangs at the ready. The instant he made eye contact it sprang out of the tree like a bolt of lightning as Bill raised his 30.06 rifle.

The bullet hit the cougar square in the chest, but it didn't even seem to slow it down. The cat's huge jaws clamped down on Bill's face, the force of the impact knocked him to the ground. He still had hold of his rifle, but he couldn't cock it, or get it into a firing position. Stunned from the fall, with the huge animal on top of him, Bill tried to use the rifle to push the cougar off him, but it ripped a chunk of flesh from his face. Quickly, it clamped its jaws down on his throat and began twisting its head back and forth. Bill put his left hand in between the cat's jaws and his throat and his right hand on the chest, pushing with all his might to get it off of him. The attack was over in seconds, the hunter laid there, muscles twitching in the throes of imminent death.

The cougar, feeling the affect of being shot in the heart, knew it was not time to eat. Slowly, it walked away until it could walk no more. The punctured heart and internal bleeding caused circulatory failure, it collapsed, looking back at Bill it closed its eyes for the last time.

Buck sat up in bed re-reading the newspaper article about the cougar hunter that was killed. When he finished he laid the paper down on the floor next to the bed and turned off the light. Marie had fallen asleep, but sleep was slow to come for him.

Swawa departed to go on a hunting trip, leaving her young behind. Normally by this age, they would accompany her and assist with the kill, but today they were all sleeping and she was hungry. While she was gone the smaller of the two male kittens began playfully batting at the bigger, mean male and it rapidly turned into a fight. When Swawa returned, without a kill, the mean male had killed the smaller one and was nearly finished eating it. Enraged she attacked him, but he was quick to defend himself and responded with a vengeance. At this, his sisters, not wanting to suffer a similar fate, joined in with the mother. Overwhelmed by numbers, he decided to flee and quickly disappeared into the forest with numerous superficial scratches.

Traveling for days, he continued to look for a home of his own. Everywhere he went there were scrapes and scratch marks on trees left by other cougars marking their territory. On the fifth day away from his family, a large eight-year old male cougar saw him walking through the woods. Weighing over one hundred eighty pounds he was a formidable adversary for any animal. He let out a scream over the nerve of another cougar in his territory and launched an attack on the intruder. The younger male was fifty yards away from his assailant, being quick and agile, he took off.

Jumping down an embankment he ran across a fallen log that went from bank to bank, creating a bridge over a large stream, and disappeared into the forest. The larger cat stayed on his side of the stream, screaming at the interloper, knowing that area belonged to another large male cougar. Not desiring a fight with the resident of that territory he sat there watching, to ensure the intruder did not return.

The mean male, now ten months old weighed eighty pounds. He continued to travel west and further down the mountain. He'd been in two fights now and was licking his wounds each night, in an attempt to fight off infection. At this age, he was really too young to be out on his own. The odds of survival were not in his favor.

He came down the mountain and followed a streambed. The farther he went down the hill the more houses he began to see. As long as he stayed next to the stream there was ample cover for him to hide from sight if it became necessary. In the next two weeks he managed to kill a few squirrels and two rabbits, but it was not nearly enough to provide him with adequate sustenance.

On day twenty-five, as he followed the flow of water he heard noises. Curious, he climbed up the side of the bank and came to a chain link fence. On the other side was a field full of children, running and playing at recess. He watched with intense curiosity, waiting for an opportunity. This prey was food, as he'd learned from his mother, but there were so many of them. Which one could he separate from the group?

Just then the bell rang, and the children all started running for their classrooms. Sarah wasn't feeling good that day and she was well behind her classmates. She was the last one to leave the grassy area, heading toward her classroom, the door open. She was forty yards behind the last of the students.

The mean male saw his chance and leaped over the six-foot high fence, from a standstill, with plenty of room to spare. He started toward her, slowly at first. Sarah was going to be late so she began to run, not knowing the cougar was a hundred yards behind her. Instinctively he took off after her, quickly closing the distance to twenty yards as she neared the classroom.

Suddenly, the students in the classroom began screaming, pointing and yelling as they looked out the window at the cougar closing in on Sarah. Mrs. Roland, their teacher, charged out the door, grabbing Sarah, pulled her close, while backing up to the door. The sudden intervention of another human, a larger one, caused the cougar to slow down. It was only a few feet away from them when Mrs. Roland slammed the door closed.

She quickly told the students to get back and away from the windows. The children were screaming as they moved away from the windows. Realizing that many of the windows were open she hastily moved from window to window, closing them, as the cougar walked along outside, watching her intently. When she closed the last one the cougar went up on his hind feet, placing both front paws on the window about four feet off the ground. Its face between the two paws looking around inside the classroom at the children, studying them as they screamed and huddled close together.

Keeping an eye on the cougar, Mrs. Roland called the office on the intercom to inform them what was going on. Claire, the office manager could barely hear what Mrs. Roland was saying because of all of the noise emanating from the classroom, but she got the part about a cougar outside the classroom. Flipping the intercom switch to all classrooms, she put a call to the other classrooms to get everyone inside, and close all the doors and windows. The principal, Mrs. Moore, a petite, but aggressive woman, came into the main office to see what was going on and heard

Claire telling everyone there was a cougar on the school grounds.

Assessing the situation quickly she said to Claire, "Call 9-1-1 and get the sheriff here as fast as possible."

Mrs. Moore was not about to have any of the children under her responsibility attacked by a cougar on her school grounds. She charged through the double glass doors to the playground, searching for any children or teachers still outside.

As she walked toward Mrs. Roland's classroom the cougar came around the corner of the building. She quickly saw it and stopped dead in her tracks. It didn't look like a real big one, maybe sixty or seventy pounds she thought, but still plenty capable of killing a person. Slowly she backed up as the cougar advanced toward her. Mr. Hartman, standing at the door of his classroom saw what was happening. Opening the door, about twenty feet from Mrs. Moore he stepped out, yelling at the cougar. He waved his arms above his head and tossed his coffee mug at it. The cougar immediately attacked the mug, slapping it away. It rattled down the asphalt and the cougar batted it again. The distraction was enough for Mrs. Moore to make a dash for the door, but when she ran, the cougar made a move to attack. Mr. Hartman closed the door just in time. The cougar stalked up and down the length of windows looking inside. He stood on his hind legs, and put his big paws up on the windows once again. Seeing all the children inside, his tongue came out and he licked his chops.

The four sheriff deputies came running from the parking lot, two had shotguns in hand. Claire pointed toward the double glass doors where a crowd had gathered to watch the suspense unfold. Spreading the crowd the four deputies walked out the door and saw the cougar looking in the windows. At the sight of the four big men with guns, the cougar dropped down and quickly disappeared around the corner of the building.

The deputies split up, two following the cat and two going around the back side of the building. When the two in direct pursuit reached the corner they saw the cougar running across the playground, heading for the woods. It was a clear shot, nothing across the playground or in the woods to be hit or damaged by a stray round, so they both fired with their shotguns. 00 buck is good knock down power at close range, but the cougar was about fifty yards away. The cougar was hit by three of the shots in the upper left rear leg, but kept on going and easily leapt over the fence, disappearing from sight into the woods. His leg was beginning to hurt as he headed back up the stream through the watershed.

The sheriff deputies were following along the stream, not far behind him. Up ahead of him was a big old maple tree, he jumped up into it, climbing about thirty feet up the tree and lay down on a huge branch. Pressing himself down close to the branch he watched as the deputies passed below him. They searched the ground and bushes intently for over an hour. When they didn't find the cougar they headed back down stream. The cougar watched them attentively. When they disappeared he began to lick his wounds.

After sunset he wrapped his front legs around the tree, then one leg at a time he placed the hind legs on the trunk and climbed down. He started working his way upstream looking for food. His left hind leg was beginning to hurt more and he had developed a slight limp. He stopped and began licking the wound. The muscle tension, along with the pressure his licking created, forced one of the 00 buck shot lodged in his leg to the surface. Pushing it aside with his nose he continued licking until the blood stopped.

About an hour later the meowing of several cats caught his attention. Following the noise out of the watershed, he ended up in Rose Towns's backyard. There were cats everywhere. Catching them by surprise he quickly snatched one. The others scattered and headed for the woods. He carried his catch behind the tool shed with the victim dangling from his jaws. Safely out of the open, he began to feed.

Rose walked out the back door of her house, carrying a bag of cat food. She loved cats and over the years had accumulated numerous strays. She took in any that wandered into her yard or that anyone just wanted to get rid of. To her surprise there were no cats to be seen anywhere.

She called, "Here kitty, kitty," but no cats appeared. Thinking this odd, she began walking around the yard looking for them.

At seventy-two years old, she had cataracts and could not see very well any more. In addition, her mind was not what it used to be. Some days she barely remembered her own name. Her husband, Bull, could not let her go anywhere on her own anymore. The last time he left her at the grocery store alone, over a year ago, while he ran some errands and was to pick her up in an hour. She got to the check-stand with a full cart of groceries and apparently could not figure out where she was and why she was there. She walked out of the store and proceeded across a busy street, against the light. Bull was sitting two cars behind the lead car at the light across the street when he realized it was Rose walking against the light. A car slammed on its brakes, stopping right against her leg as he watched in horror. He had jumped out of his car and ran to her. The traffic all stopped as he escorted her back to his car. Luckily, it was a small town where everyone watched out for their neighbors.

Rose walked around behind the tool shed and found the cougar there licking his wounds. She didn't see the carcass of the dead cat on the ground next to it. "My, you're a big kitty."

He hissed at her and she said, "It's OK. Looks like you've been injured," she tried to check out his wounds. He stood up and hissed at her again and she backed up a little.

"OK, be that way, I know what to do for an injured cat with a bad disposition." She backed away and went into the house, returning with an aerosol spray can of antibiotics.

He was laying down again licking the wounds when Rose came back, standing about three feet from him she said, "OK, this won't hurt."

He looked up at her and she sprayed a prodigious amount of the medicine on the wounds from about three feet away. Initially he was surprised at the noise, but he was feeling weak and just laid there as the soothing ointment landed on his fur. Rose found a bowl and filled it with cat food, placing it near the cougar's head. When she walked away the smell of the cat food got his attention and he got up and ate the entire bowl of food, then gingerly lay back down and began licking his wounds again.

Rose didn't say anything to Bull about the big kitty when he got home from work. She had probably forgotten about it by then anyway. Around nine that evening, Bull went out to the tool shed to get a special tool his aircraft mechanic was going to need the next day.

The noise inside the shed drew the cougar's attention and he crept around and peered inside at Bull as he looked for the necessary tool. Bull was a big man, but the cougar was still hungry, albeit weak. When Bull closed the shed door the cat was crouched at the edge of the building, concealed by darkness. It was close enough for him to touch, but he was oblivious to its presence. Walking back to the house the cougar leaped on him from behind, knocking him flat to the ground, face down. The claws of its right paw dug into his forehead, and it began chewing on his neck.

Bull yelled for all he was worth, trying to dislodge his attacker. He moved his shoulders from side to side trying to get up, but the weight of the cougar, on his eighty-year old body, proved to be too much. The cougar kept chewing on his neck trying to puncture his vertebrae. Bull gave one last heave, managing to roll over, and knock the cougar off. But it was fast to recover and was just about to clamp his huge jaws down on Bull's throat when it was suddenly whacked on the side.

Rose stood there beating on the cougar with her broom. He backed away as she yelled, "Go on, get out of here ya big brute!"

Rose was clear enough of mind to know that Bull was in trouble when she called 9-1-1. The paramedics were putting bandages on Bull's wounds and loading him into the ambulance when the sheriff's cars began to arrive. They searched all around the yard and the woods immediately behind the house, but did not find any trace of the cougar.

The next day Buck and Eric arrived at the airfield for another flight lesson. Clem informed them that Bull had been attacked by a cougar the night before and was in the hospital.

"Shall we go to the hospital and see how Bull is?" Buck asked Eric.

"Yeah."

When they arrived Bull was sitting up in bed. "Hi Bull," they both said.

"Hi Buck, Eric, how ya doin?"

"We're doing fine, how about you," Buck asked, checking out the bandages, especially the one around his head.

"Damned thing took my scalp clean off. Got plenty of scratches on my arms and back too. Nothing real serious, fortunately, but they say the infection could be a long term problem."

"How long are you going to be in here?" Eric asked.

"Another day or two. I should be back to work by next Monday."

After another half hour of conversation Buck and Eric said they'd be back for another flight next week.

Pulling out of the hospital parking lot Eric said, "Wow, he got pretty well torn up. Right in his own backyard, too."

"He was lucky Rose heard him and came to his rescue," Buck added. "It caught him by surprise. That's about the worst case scenario."

"Who'd ever guess there'd be a cougar in your back yard," Eric added.

5

Barbara Abbot was finally on her way to the long awaited backpacking trip. She'd been planning trips for months with three other women, but they always got cancelled for one reason or another. In fact, all of the others from her naturalist club that were supposed to be going with her had cancelled at the last minute on this trip.

"I'm not going to let them stop me," she said to herself, "I'm going anyway. If I put off the trip now something will happen the next time too and I'll never get to go. I want to get way out in the woods where no one else goes and do some fly-fishing." Barbara was a fiercely independent computer

engineer at a software company. Single and
financially very well off, she had the best equipment
money could buy.

She left at ten a.m. Friday morning, for the north
Cascade Mountains, arriving at the parking area near
noon. The naturalist club recommended this as one of
their best weekend backpacking trips for new hikers.
It was a five mile hike over mostly level terrain. She
unloaded the car, put her pack on, and headed up the
trail. The day was beautiful, clear and sunny, just a
tad bit on the cool side, but the sun made up for the
cool breeze. It didn't really matter, she had the right
equipment for any weather. Hiking up the trail she
took in the majesty of the mountains and the dense
forest. The heavenly scent of evergreen surrounded
her, the moment would be embedded in her memory
forever. In a short time she passed through a huge
meadow, longer than two football fields. It was so flat
it almost seemed like it had been mowed. There were
deer in groups of two to four around different areas
of the open space. She sat down to rest and observe
her surroundings. The deer didn't pay any attention
to her, even the group of four, less than forty feet
away from where she was sitting. She heard a sharp
cry and looked up to see an eagle soaring above.
Immediately, she was swept with a feeling like she
had been here before. She remembered fishing on the
Payette River, in Idaho, next to her father when she
was about ten years old. An eagle was soaring
overhead, catching the wind currents, and he had

said, "Any day you see an eagle flying, that's a lucky day."

A little after three p.m. she reached a spot that looked like a great place to camp for the weekend. The hike proved to be fairly easy for her first time out. She set up the tent, close to the river, under the cover of a huge old maple tree. After organizing her equipment she was exhausted, but anxious to get out on the river and do some fly-fishing. Finally there, in the woods, she was communicating with nature.

She sat on a rock and tied a mayfly nymph to her line, then got up and began working her way up river, casting upstream and letting the fly float downriver. If she didn't get a hit in four or five casts she'd move a little further up river to look for another good hole and repeat the process. Last summer she had taken a fly-fishing course offered by the city parks and recreation department. After that she practiced in the river near her apartment a few times. Fly fishing requires some unique skills, a lot of practice and plenty of patience. So far the fish had eluded her, but she liked the relaxation it provided, taking her mind off the problems and stress at work. Time slipped by as she whipped the tiny fly at the end of her line into the flow above a large rock so that it would float into the eddy the water created downstream of the rock or any pool deep enough that it might have a big trout laying in wait. Fly-fishing was a different challenge than spin casting or bait fishing. This method seemed more in tune with nature.

Swawa and her kittens lay sleeping, totally concealed, under the canopy of a large clump of wild rhododendrons. The plants had a dense perimeter, but inside there was plenty of room for all of them to stretch out. One of the kittens woke up and went out to stretch her legs. She went down the mountain to the river to get a drink and then continued following the trail down the river. In a short time she saw a woman standing in the river, her arms swinging back and forth. Curious, she left the trail and worked her way toward the woman, crouching down to stay concealed by the salal, salmonberry, and other low growth plants in the forest. Only fifteen feet from the woman, she sat down hidden behind a bush, watching as the woman worked the line back and forth. The woman's back was to her and the line came close to her each time as it played out for a cast. Seeing the fly on the end of the line, as it silently flew past her through the air, she began to reach out with her paw at the fly.

Barbara took in a long breath of the clean, crisp mountain air gazing at the beauty that surrounded her. Knee deep in the crystal clear, icy mountain water, she was not the least bit cold. Wearing lightweight waders over wool pants, a pair of wool socks over thinsulate socks, and a thick polarfleece top, she was both dry and warm. She was totally focused on the pool, at the base of a rock, in the middle of the river. Dropping the fly in the water, about five feet upriver from the rock with each cast, it floated around the rock into the eddy the water flow created. It was an ideal spot for a trout to be lying in the calm, where the backflow of the river would help preserve the fish's energy, and bring its next meal with the flow of the water. She pulled the line in slowly with her left hand, using the thumb and index finger, ready for the slightest hint of a strike. The excess line lay floating on top of the water near her legs until it was all the way in. Then she began working the pole back and forth letting out as much line as possible with each back-cast for a new quest.

The cougar watched closely as Barbara fed the line out, back and forth, the fly whipping near her systematically. She reached out as the fly was making its way through the air for the next round and the hook caught a tuft of fur between her claws.

Barbara flicked her pole forward, but the line was caught on the back-cast. She gave it a hard snap forward just as the cougar pulled her paw back in, snapping the thin line off right where the fly was tied to the line. The end of the line fluttered in the air before it finally hit the water, well short of its destination. Barbara didn't see the fly hit, so she pulled in the line for inspection and found the fly missing.

She made her way out of the river and sat down on the bank next to the same bush the cougar was behind. It was close enough for her to place her hand on its head, but she was unaware of the cougar's presence. As she sat there, with her back to the cougar, it sat there motionless, observing her every move while she tied a new fly on the line. When she finished she looked around, and realized the sun was about to meet the tree line. She decided it was time to head back to camp before it got too dark.

Getting up, she had a funny feeling. A shiver went up her spine. She wasn't quite sure what it was. She started walking on the trail toward her campsite, looking over her shoulder periodically. There was nothing that looked unusual, but she still felt a little uncomfortable.

The cougar slipped silently through the woods and began to stalk her from about fifty feet behind. In a short time it went deeper into the woods and ran ahead of her, finding a ledge above the trail and waited. When Barbara appeared walking down the trail toward the cat, it tensed, tail moving back and forth rapidly. As she reached the spot just below the ledge, the cougar had its ears pinned back, its muscles rippling, tail flicking back and forth rapidly, fangs exposed at the ready. At the exact instant it was ready to pounce a large black crow winging its way slowly up the river, about six feet from the surface, sounded a loud caw and broke the cougar's concentration.

Barbara continued along the trail. The moment passed and the cougar began to stalk her once again.

Barbara reached her campsite and propped her pole up against a tree. Sitting down on a big rock she removed her waders then looked back up the trail. The strange sensation was still there, like something was close, watching her. She'd never spent a night in the woods alone before, she was a little nervous. There'd been plenty of camping trips with her family when she was growing up, but those trips were always in state parks or national campgrounds. Lots of other people around, bathrooms, and piped in water. The family was big into fishing on those trips and she always enjoyed fishing next to her dad as a young girl. She hiked regularly near her home on woodsy trails and was in top physical condition. Still, being so far out here totally alone made her wonder if it had been a good idea to come by herself. It was now too close to sunset to change her mind and hike back to the car.

The cougar was about twenty feet from her, watching intently. Barbara gathered some rocks from the river's edge and made a fire pit. Picking up pieces of dead wood and pine cones around the area, she placed some small pieces in a tepee style formation, then lit it with her disposable lighter. The flame began as a flicker, but she added larger pieces until it was flaming well enough to stay lit. The fire would not only warm her up, it would also provide some sense of comfort and safety. While the fire continued to

build, she set up her little propane burner. Earlier she
had fetched a pot of water out of the river and now
she put it on the burner. Once it began boiling she
filled a water container for use later and emptied a
bag of ramen soup into what was left in the pot.
Stirring the soup until it was ready, she poured it into
a bowl, and sat down close to the fire to enjoy her
dinner. It wasn't much, but she included a roll of
French bread, sliced some cheese from a block, and
selected a plum, it was perfect.

Swawa woke up, immediately aware one of her
kittens was missing. She left the others sleeping and
departed the concealment of the rhododendron
bushes to look for her. After walking around for
about five minutes with no sign of her kitten she gave
a short cry, the call the kittens all knew as mom's call
to locate them, but the kitten was not to be found. She
returned to the other kittens and woke them up. As
the evening wore on Swawa and her offspring
searched for the missing kitten while looking for food.
They crisscrossed their way through the trees,
spreading out in a tactical hunting formation to cover
a larger area. With keen night vision they searched
the distance for movement, as they worked their way
toward the river. Instinctively, she knew deer and
other animals frequently came to the river to drink in
the early hours of the morning and evening. After
they all got a drink she walked the trail, following the

flow of the river. The kittens followed about ten feet apart. Every few minutes Swawa would give the cry again, trying to locate the wayward kitten.

The fire slowly died down to embers, and Barbara decided to call it a day. She walked over to the river and filled her pot with water to douse the fire. When she was satisfied it would not flare up she went inside the tent, zipping it closed behind her. She removed her boots, pulled the sleeping bag out of its tightly packed little stuff bag, took off her jacket and crawled in. Cold at first, her body heat promptly warmed it up. She listened for the noises of the forest, but the sound of the river was too overpowering. She was tired and sleep came quickly.

The observing adolescent cougar slowly crept up to the tent, sniffing around, she gently pressed a paw against the nylon side. Then her ears perked up, she turned away looking up the river. Listening intently she heard her mother's cry. She looked back at the tent, turned away and hurried up the river trail. As she reached her family Swawa gave her a close inspection from head to tail and licked her neck a few times. Satisfied that she was okay she turned up the mountain to continue looking for prey.

Within minutes they heard the raking clatter of a raccoon's claws coming down a tree. They homed in on the noise, crouched down, and slowly made their way toward the sound. When they located it, one of the kittens made a running jump and landed on the tree about six feet above the raccoon. The raccoon raced down the tree, keeping an eye on the cougar above, but was met by two more of the kittens near the base of the tree. It scrambled when it hit the ground, seeing the two other cougars, one was fast to attack and had it in seconds. Clamping its jaws down on the raccoon's back, the raccoon twisted around raking its sharp claws at the cat. The raccoon pulled away tufts of fur from the cat, but the cat was fast, lifting the furry animal up, twisting its head and grasping the hind quarter of the raccoon with her sharp claws she broke the raccoon's spine. It was a large raccoon, about fifty pounds, and would provide a minimal amount of sustenance for all of them for a day if no other food presented itself.

Barbara woke up to the sound of birds singing when the light of the new day hit the top of the trees. Within a few minutes she crawled out of her sleeping bag, it was chilly and she wasted no time putting on her fleece top and jacket. The thin neoprene fishing gloves she pulled on left the thumb and forefinger tips exposed on each glove. Next she slipped on her water proof boots over wool socks. Unzipping   the tent door, she lifted the flap and stepped out into the brisk morning air. She filled a pot of water from the river, set it on the butane burner, and lit it, holding her hands close to the sides to warm them up.

Knowing it would take several minutes for the water to boil, she figured she might as well make a few casts while she waited.

It was only twenty minutes after sunrise when her first cast hit the water. She felt much better about being there alone and did not have any of the feelings that she had experienced on the river last evening. She found a deep hole and decided to try a wet fly. Dropping the fly in the water about twenty feet above the pool giving it time to sink as it drifted with the flow. Holding the line between her thumb and index finger of her left hand as it drifted she felt the tiniest vibration with her fingers. She got a strike on the first try. She squeezed her fingers on the line and flicked the tip of the pole to set the hook. Holding the tip of the pole high, keeping tension on the line, she slowly pulled in the light green floating line. The fish was a fighter and she had to let some line back out to keep it from breaking off. When it was finally in close enough, she transferred the line to her right hand, pressing the line between her fingers and the grip of the pole, and scooped the fish into her net with her left hand. It was a nice fifteen inch rainbow trout.

As a child on camping trips with her parents, fishing had been a way to provide food for the table. Catch and release was okay after you had all you wanted to eat. She put it on a stringer and staked it to the bank next to her campsite. Satisfied it was securely attached, she made a cup of tea, placed some oatmeal in a cup and made herself some breakfast.

By ten she'd finished washing all the dishes and was ready to do some more fishing. Working her way upriver, she plied each pool that looked enticing. The fish were hungry and she'd managed to get numerous scrappy fighters on the line, but for various reasons she had yet to get another one into her creel. In spite of it, she was having the time of her life. Hours later she became aware that the light was beginning to fade. She decided it was time to call it quits. Pulling in the line she felt another twitch between her left thumb and index finger. Flicking the tip of the pole she'd hooked another. This one was a real fighter. It jumped four times before she had it next to her side, scooping it into her net. This one was a beautiful sixteen inch long brown trout. Placing it in her creel she headed back to camp.

On arrival she pulled the fish out of the creel and took a good long look. This was one of the nicest fish she had ever caught, placing it on the stringer with the other to have for dinner. She got the campfire going and cleaned the fish, leaving the head and guts in the river for small fish to feed on. She admired the fish as she sat by the fire cooking them in an open pan.

It smelled wonderful and reminded her of her youth when the family spent weeks on camping trips. Back in those days by the end of the second week they were running low on supplies, and there were no stores nearby. In fact, the nearest store was probably seventy miles away. As the weeks wore on they ate more and more trout. By the end of the third week they were eating trout for breakfast, lunch and dinner. She remembered Mom cooking them different ways trying to make it seem like it was something new. One such culinary delight was on a trip to northern Idaho when she dipped the trout in flour and then sprinkled them with cinnamon. It actually tasted pretty good, but backpacking was different. Space was at a premium, she had no flour or cinnamon on this trip. Plus, these were the first trout she'd had for a long time, they were delicious.

In the twilight, just before sunset, Swawa and her kittens were walking, single file, along a game trail when she caught the odor of fish, wafting through the forest. Her senses perked up immediately. She moved her head from one side to the other trying to determine the direction of the delectable odor. In the woods it was difficult to find the source and direction of an odor. Sensing the direction of the breeze she began to move down the hill toward the river. The kittens followed her at a spacing of twenty to thirty feet. They reached the river trail and the breeze was coming up the river. There were many odors blending into the air and the moisture near the river diluted the scent. Turning her head one way then the other, she turned to follow the trail down the river. The aroma was faint at first, but the smell of the cooking fish became stronger as they followed the river's flow down the dark trail. Their keen night vision spotted the campfire in the distance.

Barbara buried the fish remains, washed and dried the dishes, then put everything in the pack. By the time she finished it was dark, and there was really nothing else to do, so she put out the fire and retired to the tent. It had been a long day, but she felt great about being out on her own. The fishing was nothing less than spectacular. The only thing that could have made it better would've been a companion to share this experience. Hopefully, next time she'd have her friends along.

Comfortable in the relative safety of the tent, she took off her jacket, boots, and top shirt and crawled into her sleeping bag. Staring at the top of the tent she reminisced of the camping trips she'd been on as a young girl and then thought out her plan for tomorrow. She'd get up early, fish until about ten, then pack everything up, and hike out about noon. In her mind she figured she'd be home around five. The sound of the water moving down the river basin obliterated all other moderate sounds of the forest and she was lulled to sleep in a short time.

Near one a.m. she awoke to a sound outside the tent. Startled, she realized there was something out there. She lay still, listening. A minute later she heard a twig break next to the tent. The moonlight was just enough to see the outline of the tent and what appeared to be a shadow cast on the side of the tent. Something was pushing on the tent. It was so close to her she could hear it breathing. Faint at first, but as she became more acutely aware of it, when she realized, it was not a small animal. Maybe it was a bear she thought. She was petrified with fear, unable to move.

Swawa put her paw on the side of the tent and gently pushed. It yielded no resistance, it seemed there was nothing there. She pushed her claws out and penetrated through the woven nylon material into the tent, nothing. She retracted her claws, moving her paw to a different area of the tent and repeated the process several times, still nothing. In the dim light of the moon, Barbara lay there watching as the claws came in and out of the tent.

She was horror stricken, but didn't dare make a sound. Swawa put her paw back on the ground, making her way completely around the tent two times, studying the edges, looking for a way in. She couldn't figure it out and let out a loud hiss, a tactic used by cougars when trying to flush a hidden animal out into the open. Apparently this method works because it's a fairly common cougar behavior. Barbara was holding her breath, about to pass out when the hiss came. It was so close it caused Barbara to gasp for air. Swawa heard the sound and batted the side of the tent. Barbara rolled away just in time to keep the tent wall from pressing against her shoulder. Soon there were paws pressing on all sides of the tent, but when they felt no resistance they backed away to quietly watch the tent.

Thirty minutes later, Barbara relaxed slightly when there had been no sound of activity outside. Thinking more clearly, she moved her hand slowly to her backpack and withdrew her folding knife, opened it and clutched it tightly in her hand. 'What now?' she thought. Around four a.m., there had been no more sounds outside for a long time, exhausted from stress she slipped into a deep sleep.

Swawa and her kittens gave up the quest in the middle of the night, but she knew there was something inside the unique enclosure. They all found a comfortable spot under a nearby fir tree and went to sleep.

Slowly, light began to wake the day creatures of the forest. Barbara awoke to the sounds of birds singing in the trees above her. Opening her eyes with quiet trepidation, she laid still, listening. There were no unusual sounds so she gingerly, unzipped her sleeping bag and crawled out, careful not to make any noise. Silently she lifted the flap of the window just slightly and looked out. Everything appeared normal. Little by little she unzipped the door enough to look around the front of the tent, nothing. She closed the door and zipped it back closed for reassurance and sat in the middle of the tent. Relief flooded over her, thinking, it was all just a bad dream.

She sat there, propped up against her backpack, for another half an hour trying to relax and regain her composure. Convinced that it had just been a nightmare she unzipped the door and crawled out with the backpack. Standing up she quickly looked around in all directions, everything seemed to be normal. She propped the backpack up against a tree and went over to the fire pit, still a little uneasy. Yesterday she'd gathered kindling and put it into a plastic bag to keep it dry from the night dew. She took some out and placed it in a small mound in the fire pit and began to get the fire going.

Swawa stretched when she woke to the smell of smoke. Nudging her kittens, they all moved silently toward the camp.

Barbara was beginning to feel much better. The fire was going and she had water boiling to make tea and oatmeal. She picked up her fly-rod and examined it. Looking at the river to see if there were any fish coming to the surface, she heard a branch snap behind her. Fear washed over her, but it came and went quickly. Surely it was nothing. Just in case she got up slowly and turned around. A large cougar and three smaller ones were coming straight at her. Grabbing the backpack she held it above her head, yelling and screaming as she shook the pack. The cougars continued toward her undeterred. Barbara threw the backpack at the biggest one when they were only ten feet away. It caused them all to jump back. The distraction it created bought her a couple of seconds. She bolted inside the tent quickly zipping it closed, and grabbed the knife.

The cougars circled the tent and began hissing. It was no nightmare, it really happened, and they were back. It was much worse than a nightmare, this was for real.

Suddenly the sides of the tent were under siege. As the cats walked around the perimeter of the tent their long tails swung back and forth, whacking the sides of the tent from all directions. The thin nylon material yielded no resistance. Barbara held the knife so tightly her knuckles were white. She was drenched in sweat as the siege went on periodically for over an hour.

Unable to make contact the cougars backed off, sat down, and watched the tent. Barbara sat in the center of the tent, waiting, but nothing happened. Time for a new plan, time to get the hell out of there, but how? Looking up at the tent window she raised the flap about an inch. She could see the river trail, and no cougars were in sight. The tent was a small light weight dome, six feet by six feet. She took the knife and cut two straight lines, eighteen inches long and parallel to each other, in the floor of the tent. When she was finished she attached the metal clip on the side of the knife to the outside edge of her front pocket, still locked open. Barbara put one boot through each hole, looked out the flap quickly to get a mental picture of the trail, and gripped two opposing dome stays with her hands. She lifted the tent off the ground and began walking in the blind. After about ten steps the cougars were all around the tent trying to figure out this new development. Some batted at the sides, others began to hiss. After about twenty steps she stopped and let the tent down.

Her arms were aching from holding them up, but she didn't like the cat's paws on the side of the tent, it could be torn open too easily. If they could see her she was doomed. It was also vital for her to stay on the trail. Gingerly she raised the window flap and made mental calculations to get back on the trail. She could see one of the cougars, but fortunately it was not looking at her. Eye contact would likely result in an instant attack.

As she put the tent down to rest the cougars stopped and studied it. A paw poked once again at the side of the tent. Scared, she quickly grabbed the stays and resumed walking. One of the kittens swatted under the tent floor. A claw caught the heel of her boot and tripped her, causing her to fall to her knees. The force of the blow ripped the heel right off the boot. Quickly she got back up, determined to keep moving.

An hour after she headed out toward her car it began to rain. It was a light mist at first, but as it grew in intensity, it made the trail muddy and slippery. Soon the rain turned heavier, eventually becoming a downpour. She was soaking wet with sweat, both from the exertion and from the nerve-racking experience. Worn out, she collapsed in the center of the tent.

She opened her eyes. How long had she been out? Her watch was in the backpack, back at the campsite. She was muddy from the waist down and there was mud all over the tent floor. Raising the window flap, ever so slowly, she saw two cougars laying down, facing her, their eyes were closed. That was fortunate. Getting her bearings she looked around, seeing that she was still on the trail, then in the distance, she saw her car. Flush with emotion, she thrust up the tent and began to run for the car. The cats were all over her, swinging at her feet and brushing against the side of the tent. She stopped immediately and let the tent down, the attack ceased simultaneously. What was she thinking? She was so close, but running was a bad idea. She sat there in the center of the tent and tried to relax, calm her emotions and think clearly. Picking up the tent imperceptibly, she inched her way to the car. The cats belly crawled along side the tent, watching it closely. Twenty minutes later she was at the driver's side of the car.

That was when it hit her, like a ton of bricks landing on her. The keys were in the backpack, back at the campsite. She crumpled in the center of the tent, and wanted to cry, but she couldn't. Her willpower wouldn't allow it. Think! Suddenly she remembered there was a key hidden under the passenger side of the car inside a magnetic metal box, attached to the frame. She lifted the tent with renewed vigor and inched her way around the car to the other side. Pressing the tent door up against the door of her

BMW convertible, she unzipped the tent door just enough to get her arm through and under the passenger side of the car. The tent conformed to the side of the car and engulfed the car door. Lying down on her back, she pushed her arm through all the way to her shoulder, and ran her hand around until she found the small metal box.

One of the kittens sensed movement under the car and thrust its head under the driver's side. The cat's loud scream pierced the air. Swinging its paw frantically, it missed Barbara's hand by mere inches. It wriggled hysterically trying to close the distance, but the space between the ground and the car frame was too narrow for the cougar to get any closer to her.

Terrified, Barbara could see the paw swinging, feeling the breeze as it passed through the air, only inches from her hand. She grasped the key box in a death grip and pulled it inside, zipping the door closed. There was a lot of cat activity now, she sensed them moving around, agitated. There wasn't much time. She got up quickly, leaning her shoulder against the passenger door, the tent wall in between, and gripped the key box in both hands. They were all hissing and screaming now at this new development. She slid the box open and held the key in her right hand. So close, but not out of the woods yet. Now what? How do I get out of the tent and into the car?

One of the kittens jumped on the roof of the car and let out a loud hiss. The resilient surface of the convertible top left the cat with unsteady footing. It jumped off the roof of the car and onto the top of the tent, but quickly rolled off.

Panic struck, the frontal assault brought Barbara to action. She pressed the tent up against the passenger door, unzipped the tent door about twelve inches and unlocked the car door. Putting her left foot on the floor at the bottom of the zipper she held her left hand against the top of the zipper, pressing it against the trailing edge of the car door and pulled the zipper open about thirty inches. She pulled the car door open just enough and hastily slid from the tent to the inside of the car.

Sensing the action inside the tent one of the kittens jumped on top of the car. As the tent fell away the cat saw her moving from the tent to the inside of the car. Swinging its paw at the closing door a claw was trapped between the window and the rubber molding as the door pulled shut. It let out an ear piercing scream as it pulled and tugged trying to free its claw.

Barbara crawled over into the driver's seat. Fumbling to get the key into the ignition the cougars could see her now. Two were on the hood in a flash, staring through the windshield at her, screaming, fangs dripping with saliva. The cougar on the roof finally pulled its claw away from the door, breaking off the tip in the process. It let out another scream. The instant the car started, Barbara slammed it into reverse, stomping on the gas as she turned the steering wheel. The two cats were thrown off the hood, the one on the roof dug its claws through the canvas roof. She could see the claws beginning to tear the material. As soon as she hit the brakes the two cats were back on the hood staring through the windshield with fire in their eyes. She thrust the car into drive and floored it. The two on the hood were thrown off again, but the big one was right at the driver's door, running along side keeping pace with the car, looking right at her with fierce determination in her eyes. As Barbara gained speed they all trailed behind her, except the one on the roof. It pulled its claws through the canvas top and tore a gaping hole.

A huge paw was thrust through the hole in the roof. The first pass missed her head by mere inches. Panicked, she slammed on the brakes. The cougar flew over the hood, landing on its feet, spun around, and came back at her. She floored it again, heading directly at the cat. The cougar jumped straight up, springing from all fours simultaneously, landing on the canvas top of the car. The speed caused it to loose its footing immediately, and it rolled off the trunk lid. Barbara looked in the rear view mirror, relief washed over her when she saw it rolling on the road.

Speeding down the mountain, she had a death grip on the steering wheel. The cats gave up the chase as the speed of the car quickly left them behind. Accelerating down the highway an approaching curve in the road caused her to look at the speedometer, ninety miles per hour. She took her foot off the accelerator and applied the brake with enough force to slow the car down before the curve. She was sweating profusely, and in need of a drink of water, but the adrenalin was pumping and kept her going.

Finally she reached the bottom of the mountain and found herself in a small town. Around other people now, she began to relax. Waiting at a stop light she saw a small café across the street, and realized she needed a break. The light turned green and she pulled into the parking lot of the café and went inside. Picking an empty booth next to a window, a waitress came over and set down a glass of water. Barbara ordered hot earl grey tea. Slightly shaking she drank the whole glass of water before the young woman returned with the tea. After the waitress left she wrapped both hands around the cup. She wasn't cold, but her hands were trembling enough to spill the tea. In the booth next to her sat Rick Dance.

Buck and Eric had just finished a flight and stopped at the café for a burger. When they walked into the cafe they spotted Rick sitting by himself.

"Hi Rick, mind if we join you?"

"Hi Buck, Eric," he said shaking hands with them. "Have a seat."

"Thanks again for helping us get the plane out of the rut and get it back in the air."

"Glad to be of assistance. What's new with you two?"

Eric announced, "I'm going cougar hunting. You've been around cougars for a long time. Do you have any advice for me?"

"Yes, don't do it."

Barbara overheard the comment and turned around. "I know where you can find four of them today. I just had the most terrifying experience of my life!"

"I'm Rick Dance, a biologist with the forest service, and I'm a cougar researcher. I'd like to hear your story, if you don't mind. Would you care to join us?"

She thought for a minute. He was wearing a ranger's uniform, and she thought 'why not'. She needed to tell someone what happened and he seemed like the right person.

"Sure," and moved over to their table.

After telling the story Rick said, "Well, that's one for the books. You're a lucky lady, also very resourceful. Sounds like your ingenuity probably saved your life. If you don't mind I'd like to get your name and number so I can report this to the state fish and wildlife officer that covers that area. We've known each other for years. I'm sure he'll also be interested to hear what happened. He'll need to go up there and check things out. I'll most likely go along with him."

They all said their 'good byes' outside the café and headed off in their own directions.

On arrival at home Barbara walked from the garage into the kitchen, picked up her portable phone, took off her clothes and slipped into a hot bubble bath with a big glass of white wine. Cozy in the bath she took a drink of the wine and called her best friend, the one that had not been able to make the trip, and told her the whole story.

Rick called Greg Spencer and both agreed to meet at the site parking area in two hours. They figured the trail might be narrow so instead of taking 4x4 ATV's they decided to take horses. Rick arrived shortly before Greg and was taking his horse, Rusty, out of the trailer when Greg's state truck pulled in towing a horse trailer. As soon as Greg parked, his dogs became agitated, they already had the scent. Greg got his horse out of the trailer, saddled it up, and turned the dogs loose. The dogs were well ahead of them, but in the woods the dogs would tree the cat or in this case cats. They'd have time to get to them once they heard the telltale 'treed cat' baying of the dogs.

Cougars frequently use game trails, people trails, logging roads or other paths to make traveling easier, and to give them the advantage of being able to see unsuspecting prey farther off in the distance. They especially like railroad tracks and the areas that have been cleared below major power transmission lines. The dogs had taken off up the same trail that Barbara had used. Rick and Greg quickly mounted up and trotted up the trail in pursuit.

"That was a pretty scary experience the woman had. Must have been her lucky day," Greg said. "Do you think it's all true?"

"Well, it didn't take the dogs long to get the scent, so I'd guess at least some of it was. She seemed pretty shaken and straight forward when she was telling us what happened."

"This will be one for the records. I'll call her when I get back and take a report."

They talked as they headed in the direction of the barking dogs. Suddenly about an hour after they left the parking area the pitch of the howling dogs increased and they were running at full speed.

Swawa and her kittens were sleeping under a big spruce tree when they heard the dogs. Quickly they headed up the side of the mountain, away from the barking dogs. Traveling through the woods, the mother searched for a big tree as they began to lose ground. Stopping, she looked in the direction of the barking, she could see them now. She leapt up into a big cedar tree and the kittens followed. Soon the dogs were at the base of the tree, baying 'treed cat'. Rick and Greg were about a mile from the dogs when they heard the long howling cries.

The mother and her kittens were thirty-five feet up the tree. She and one of the kittens were so far from the ground they were obscured from the dog's vision by the branches. It was a densely wooded area and there were many trees with overlapping branches, especially higher up. Swawa jumped over to the branch of an adjacent tree and went down the back side, hidden from the dogs. One of her offspring followed. The dogs were so busy jumping and baying at the base of the original tree they were completely unaware Swawa and a kitten were now behind them.

As one of the dogs backed up for another run at the tree, Swawa moved in on him. She swung her right paw into the hind leg of the dog with so much force the dog went flying into the air, crashing into the trunk of a tree. Dazed from the blow it was slow to move after it hit the ground. Swawa was on him instantly. Grabbing it by the back and the chest with her claws, she began chomping at the back of his neck until her canine fangs sliced through between two vertebrae. When the fangs penetrated the spinal cord the fluid began to leak out, reducing the fluid that surrounds the brain and protects it from injury. Without the spinal fluid the brain banged around inside the cranium, causing the dog intense pain.

The cougar continued chewing on its neck and shaking the dog until the spinal cord was so damaged the dog went limp, paralyzed. One of the other dogs saw what was happening and went after Swawa, but the kitten was faster, pouncing on the dog from behind it and had the back of his head in her jaws before it reached the mother. The cat picked the dog up off the ground, swung it around, crushing its skull and breaking its neck simultaneously.

The other kittens watched from above. They quickly began moving down the tree when they saw Swawa and the kitten attack the two dogs. The other two dogs sensed something was happening and turned around. Immediately they took off for the two cats on the ground. One of the kittens in the tree leaped onto the back of one dog. Digging her claws deep into its back, she rolled over on her side and Swawa lunged at it, grasping it by the throat. Her jaws clamped down, twisting her head back and forth violently, reaching a paw over the dog's head she dug in her claws and gave a downward thrust, breaking its neck. The last kitten jumped from the tree to the ground and attacked the remaining dog. It came from behind grasping the head in its jaws, another tore into the underbelly with its right front paw. The claws ripped a gash in the stomach. As the dog continued to fight, the muscular contractions caused the intestines to be exuded out. The dog continued to put up a fight until Swawa came in from the side. Grasping the neck she lifted it off the ground and gave it a flinging twist, breaking its neck. Two of the kittens tore into the chest cavity, one took the heart, the other took the liver.

The fight was over, and the cats stood over the dead and dying dogs, licking the still warm blood. There was enough there to feed all of them for a few days.

Rick and Greg noticed the change in the sound of the dogs barking, not knowing they were fighting the cougars. The dogs gradually stopped barking completely. This was not a good sign. Greg began to gallop when he first heard the barking change to fighting sounds, and Rick followed suit. The noise from the horse's hooves got Swawa's attention. Reluctant to leave all this food behind, she sensed danger in the increasing intensity of the sound heading in their direction. She made a short, sharp cry of danger to her kittens and took off at a full run. In a few minutes she found a huge maple tree and jumped up into it, climbing about forty feet up the tree. The kittens followed her. There was one branch large enough for three of them, Swawa chose one for herself. They could see the dead dogs lying on the ground, but they were well camouflaged by the leaves of the tree and from the distance they were nearly invisible.

Greg saw the dogs laying on the ground when they rounded a bend in the trail. His heart almost stopped.

"No!" he yelled. He'd had a sinking feeling when the dogs stopped barking, they were either seriously wounded or dead. Greg drew out his Colt .45 semi-automatic and chambered a round.

They both got off their horses to check the dogs, each had a broken neck or back. Rick examined each dog carefully, they all had a lot of puncture wounds on the back and one had been disemboweled and partly eaten. Rick hadn't brought his dog, Goldie, because he wasn't sure how the dogs would all get along. He was glad now.

"What I'm seeing here is pretty typical of a cougar kill site," Rick noted. "Considering the time frame from when the baying turned to fighting, then stopped completely, I'd say there has to be more than one. It only took us ten to fifteen minutes to get here after the barking stopped."

Greg began looking around the area, first at ground level, then up in the trees. He looked straight at the tree the cougars were in, but saw nothing. Rick carried a twelve-gauge shotgun on his saddle in the event of an unavoidable bear or cougar attack and drew it out of the sheath checking to make sure it was loaded, he chambered a round and put the safety on. Rick loved studying cougars. Having to shoot one was not something he wanted to do. However, having one on his back, chewing on his head was even less appealing.

They both walked around the area together looking for signs, walking directly under the tree the cougars lay in. Swawa and her kittens watched intently, silently. Greg looked up into the tree. It was a large one with lots of big, thick branches. Vision was good to about twenty feet up, but after that it became increasingly obscured by the branches and foliage.

"It's going to be dark in a little over an hour."

"Yeah, I was just thinking that myself. Pretty likely they're around somewhere," still looking up into the tree, his gun extended above his head, following his eyes. "Let's keep looking for another thirty minutes. Without dogs it's going to be pretty hard to find them."

When darkness was imminent Greg said, "Let's find a good spot where we can hide, but still see the dogs, and stake it out."

"Sounds like a good plan. Cougars almost always stay near a fresh kill and come back later to feed. They probably heard us coming and took off."

They led the horses around until they found a small stand of younger trees. Some of the branches hung low enough to the ground they could sit or lay down and not be noticed. They took the horses behind the trees about fifty feet away and tied them to a tree that would keep them out of view from the direction of the dead dogs. Both took their camouflage color sleeping bags off the back of the saddle.

"Might as well stay warm and concealed,"

"Yeah, could be a long night," Rick answered.

Swawa and the kittens watched every move they made. She watched as they sat down on the ground and pulled the bags up around themselves. They would have been difficult to see if she hadn't watched them move into that position.

At two in the morning the men sat sleepily staring at the dead dogs. There had been no activity anywhere around the area all night. Swawa gave a motion for her kittens to stay there. She climbed down to the ground, quietly moving through the trees until she was directly behind the two men. Crouched down low to the ground, she focused on the two humps sitting under the low tree branches. After about fifteen minutes Rusty, Rick's horse, caught her scent. He blew a quick blast of air out his nostrils and began stamping his feet. Greg's horse let out a long whinny.

Rick and Greg knew immediately what this meant, something the horses feared was near. They both threw off the bags and began looking around, holding their guns at the ready. Swawa was well concealed in the dark, crouching down behind a fallen log. The men stayed side by side and moved toward the horses, walking within ten feet of her. They patted the horse's heads to calm them, the distraction giving her an opportunity to silently slip away into the darkness. Sensing the cougar had left, the horses began to relax.

Swawa jumped back up into the tree and climbed up to the kittens. When she was sure they were all there she lay down on the big branch and went to sleep. At the break of dawn Swawa opened her eyes for a quick appraisal of the situation. The two humps were still there next to the tree.

The lack of activity lulled Rick and Greg to sleep around four. When the sun peeked over the horizon it brought activity to the forest. The sharp cry of a stellar jay woke Greg up first. Looking at the dead dogs, they appeared to be unchanged, so he nudged Rick. "Guess we'd better call for some back-up dogs and some more help."

"Sounds like a good plan to me. I'll heat up some water for coffee and get us some granola bars out of the horse pack."

Greg took out his cell phone. "No reception here, figures."

They sat next to the burner, to take off the morning chill, and drank their coffee. "We might as well head back to the trucks, we'll need to meet the reinforcements there anyway. I'll keep trying with the phone as we travel."

Riding back to the trucks, Rick thought about the chain of events of the last day. Initially he came with Greg because of the unusual circumstances of what happened to Barbara. Cougar behavior was his specialty, and the behavior patterns were certainly changing. Now that the dogs had been killed the new hunting party would be out for blood. He didn't want any part of that. He'd kill one in self-defense, but not this way.

Arriving at the trucks, the cell phone still didn't have any reception. Greg started his truck and used the radio to call for assistance. The arrival time for two officers and four more dogs would be two to three hours.

Greg had a feeling Rick might not want to be a part of it all. "You don't need to go back out with us if you don't want to."

"I was just thinking that I've got some work that needs to get done. Guess I'll head out."

"I appreciate you going out with me. I always enjoy your company."

"Sure, when it's all over, give me a call and fill me in on the details. This has been a pretty unusual case."

"Well do."

Rick put Rusty in the trailer, shook Greg's hand, and was on his way.

Fifteen minutes after the two men on horseback were out of sight, Swawa and her kittens instinctively knew it was safe. Descending out of the tree, they went straight to the dogs and began to feed. Two hours later, one by one, they lay down and took a nap.

Rocky and Tim, the reinforcements, arrived and unloaded their horses. Tim took the dogs out of the kennels, attached each one to individual leashes that were connected to a long leash. Tim mounted his horse when they were all ready, holding onto the leash. He'd keep the dogs tethered until they got to the site. It was long enough for the dogs to have some running space next to the horse as he rode. Greg told them the whole story along the way. He also warned them to stay close to the dogs once they let them loose. Hopefully they could avoid a repeat of the incident the day before. The dogs got the scent right away and pulled at the lead, but Tim held on tight.

A little after two in the afternoon the cougars woke to the sound of dogs barking in the distance. The same sounds they'd heard yesterday. Swawa knew immediately it was another potential meal, but also understood there was danger. She took the kittens, moving to a ridge where they could see the dead dogs and the trail that led up to the carcasses.

Lying down, they watched and listened. When they came into view the dogs were close to the three horsemen. She didn't like the way this looked, but laid there waiting.

The closer they got the more excited the dogs became. The officers dismounted when they arrived at the site and examined the remains. The dogs did the same, sniffing at the almost wholly consumed dogs. The only parts of the remains left intact were the heads and feet. Smelling around the area they picked up the strong scent of the cougars. Greg drew his gun and held it at his side as they looked around the area.

"It looks like they came back. There must be four or more of them to have eaten this much in only a few hours. I should have thought about the possibility they were out of sight watching us, just waiting for us to leave. Under the circumstances I didn't think we had much chance of finding them and I didn't have the feeling that Rick really wanted to be there. In the event of a problem I'd rather have professional back-up."

The dogs continued to pull at the leashes as they sniffed around.

Tim said, "Let's turn the dogs loose and go after them."

Greg and Rocky got on their horses as Tim released the dogs. All four of them sat down.

"Go get'em," Tim demanded. The dogs just sat there. He nudged the one that was usually the leader with the toe of his boot, "go on," but it just sat there.

"Well this is just great," Rocky said. "Leave them loose and let's ride around to see if we can find any sign of the cats. Maybe the dogs will change their minds and get into the game."

They all drew out their Colt .45's and started riding about twenty feet apart. They looked up in the trees and around the general area. Swawa and her kittens lay silently, unmoving, watching the officers. Greg was disappointed after two hours of searching without finding even the slightest indication of the cats.

"We'll never find them without the dogs," Greg said. "Let's go get them and ride up the trail a ways and give them another try."

They went back to the kill site and the dogs were all sitting there at full attention, looking around, sniffing the air.

Tim put the dogs back on the leashes and they rode up the trail about a mile. The dogs continued sniffing all the way, but never set off or pulled on their leashes. Tim got off his horse and let the dogs off the leashes. They walked around the area sniffing at everything. About five minutes later they returned to Tim's side and sat down, refusing to move.

"These dogs aren't going to help us any. Let's head back to the kill site and give the dead dogs a decent burial. There isn't enough left of them to interest the cougars in coming back tonight."

Once they got back to the site, they scanned the area again without anything interesting turning up. Each took an entrenching tool off their horse packs and buried the dogs' remains.

It was beginning to get dark when they arrived at the horse trailers. It didn't take long to get the horses and dogs loaded up.

Greg shook hands with Tim and Rocky. "Thanks for coming out, sorry it worked out this way. I'll go back to the station and brief the sergeant about what happened. It's probably a dead issue at this point unless he wants to try some different dogs. By tomorrow the trail will probably be too old for a good chase and I'm too exhausted to try again tonight."

Photo by Lee Dygert

6

The cats were all sprawled out together under the cover of a huge cedar tree, the branches slung low to the ground. It was a rainy afternoon, a week after they had eaten the tracking dogs. They'd roamed around Swawa's home range all week and were unable to find any kind of game. Four months ago they were able to kill a deer almost every day. There were few game animals in Swawa's home range now because they had systematically, one by one, eaten most of them and those that were left were hard to find. In some sectors of her range all of the game had been consumed, every living creature except the birds. Even some of the birds had succumbed to the wily hunting skills of the kittens. Swawa had taught them to lie still in a tree and wait for the birds to come to them. Not much of a meal, but it improved their dexterity. All of them were masters at the waiting game. Even the birds were difficult to find now. New animals would eventually come back into all areas, but it took time for that to happen. As the kittens grew older, they ate more.

The west side of Swawa's home range was near a housing development. In the past she'd stayed well away from the area because she realized that there was potential danger near large numbers of people. Hungry, she took her kittens west. In the early evening they came to a trail in the watershed that bordered the houses. The watershed was about two hundred yards wide and had a small stream that conveyed rain and water run off from the area bordering the houses until it reached other watersheds and turned into a continuous stream on the way to the Puget Sound. A picturesque foot trail worked its way along side the stream among the firs, cedar, maples, alders and numerous different types of shrubs. Some of the trees were nearly a hundred feet high.

Walking down the trail she heard something, it was people coming toward them on the trail. She looked around and quickly found a small game trail going into a huge patch of blackberry bushes. She crawled inside and the kittens followed her. Soon there was a man, a woman and two children passing them. They all crouched down, silent, motionless, watching. The people passed them totally unaware of their presence. When they were well out of sight the cats emerged and continued on the trail.

Before long they heard more noise. This time it was approaching fast. They all jumped off the trail and found what cover they could. There wasn't much to hide them this time because of the short notice. None of them were concealed very well. They all crouched down and waited motionlessly. Two young boys appeared on bicycles riding down the trail yelling at each other as they passed the cats. One of the kittens jumped out from hiding and began chasing the last bicycle. Swawa quickly gave a short, sharp cry and the kitten stopped, turned around and returned, joining the others who were walking the trail again in the opposite direction. Neither of the boys saw or heard the cougar chasing them. Even though they viewed humans as prey now, Swawa was smart enough to know that there were too many of them around.

As the light grew dim Swawa saw a man walking the trail alone toward them. A big maple tree was next to the trail and she jumped straight up into it, the kittens following suit. There were several large branches big enough to support them. She selected one directly over the trail about fifteen feet off the ground and lay down flat, watching the man approach. In the daylight she would have been easily visible, but in the dying light she blended into the surroundings. More importantly, the man was looking at the trail, not up in the trees. Her offspring were on different branches about ten feet away from her, pressing tight against the branches. The lone man carried a sturdy walking stick as he passed underneath her, close enough to touch her with the stick, but he was oblivious to their presence. She didn't like the look of the stick as she closely watched him continue on down the trail. Then came more sounds of people on the trail. They stayed in the tree until it became dark and the people stopped coming past.

Dropping out of the tree Swawa continued up the trail again until she found a smaller game trail going into some dense brush, the opening about the size of a basketball. Inspecting it and sniffing around the edges, she could tell that the trail was used regularly. Most small wild animals are creatures of habit. Whatever animals were using it would probably travel through the area about the same time every day, or more likely at night. She backed off, found cover and waited.

Around midnight a very large raccoon emerged and headed down the main foot trail. It was not paying much attention to its surroundings. Living this near to humans had kept the animals in relative safety from carnivorous predators, and led them to become careless. Swawa leapt out of hiding, took two long strides and swung her claw with enough force to knock the raccoon off the trail, but her claws dug in deep and held fast. The raccoon screamed, then hissed loudly, but she quickly clamped her jaws down on its head and flicked her head back and forth in rapid succession, quickly, breaking its neck.

There was a small population of raccoons and possum in the watershed. The cats managed to catch something in the early morning and evening each day for a week. Once they had their catch they dragged it back up into the woods well away from the houses. Swawa was smart enough to know that if they stayed in the watershed to consume their catch, eventually their presence would be discovered by people. If the skeletons of their kills were found, the humans would become suspicious that something was in the watershed that maybe shouldn't be there.

A week had passed in the watershed, even a large raccoon every day was not enough to feed them all. Fighting erupted at each meal over feeding rights, they needed more food. Swawa motioned for her kittens to stay behind in the cover of the trees and she emerged from the watershed on the side of the houses.

Crouching low to the ground, in the long grass, she saw three deer eating roses next to the front porch of a house. Apparently the deer stayed in the housing area all the time. They had not seen any evidence of deer in the watershed all week. She inched her way through the tall grass until she reached a point where the grass suddenly was short and it would no longer conceal her. She stayed just out of sight, hugging the ground, watching the deer. There were people in some of the yards near the houses. Occasionally a car drove past, she watched them too, but was more interested in the deer.

If she gave chase to the deer, surely the people would see. Not likely she could get any of them without being seen by at least one of the people. Then she'd have to drag it away. After a time the deer moved on to the next house and went out of Swawa's sight. She didn't dare follow them in the daylight.

When darkness fell she summoned her kittens with a short sharp cry. They all walked over to where she had first seen the deer, following their path around the house and moving on to the next one. They roamed around the whole neighborhood looking for the deer, but found none.

Around eleven they were walking behind a six-foot high cedar fence. Dogs suddenly began barking furiously on the other side of the fence. The barking dogs stayed with them as they walked. Swawa jumped up on the flat two by four that capped the top of the fence. Three full grown rottweilers backed up when they saw the cougar, but they continued to snarl and bark. The kittens also jumped up on top of the fence and two of the dogs began to back up farther.

Swawa leapt off the fence, landing five feet in front of the last dog. When it lunged at her, she deftly swung her paw, connecting with its front right leg. Her claws dug deep through its muscles yielding two inch slashes before the weight of its body caused it to disengage, flinging it into the fence. Swawa was on it immediately, grabbing it by the back of the neck in her jaws. The dog twisted and fought, freeing itself from her grasp. Torn and bleeding from the leg and neck it was enraged. It came back at her, but one of the kittens jumped off the fence and swung its claws into the dog's right rear hind quarter, flipping the weakened dog onto its side. Swawa was fast, clamping her jaws on its throat. She lifted it off the ground and twisted her head to the side as the dog's front legs pawed at her chest. She slammed it down to the ground on its back to get the front paws away from her. The kitten slashed its claws into the dog's soft underside, and with a forceful thrust disemboweled it.

Jake Williams and his wife were sitting in the living room watching TV when the dogs started barking. This was not unusual, in fact it happened regularly. When the barking stopped abruptly, after only a couple of minutes, it got Jake's attention. Sometimes they would bark for an hour. Jake decided he should go out back to check it out.

The other two dogs had their backsides pressed against the back door. They sat there cowering as the remaining two kittens dropped off the fence, joined by the third, advancing toward them. When the cats were fifteen feet from the dogs the back door light came on. The kittens jumped off to the side out of sight just when the door opened. The dogs quickly bolted into the house. Jake looked out into the backyard to see a cougar licking blood from the coat of his favorite dog.

He raised his arms and yelled at the big cat. Swawa looked up at the man and hissed, taking a step toward him.

Jake quickly closed the door and yelled, "Where's my gun?" running to his bedroom. "There's a cougar in the back yard and it's got Bandit." He grabbed his 9 mm semi-automatic pistol out of the bedside stand.

Swawa sensed danger when the back door closed. She took the back of the limp dog's neck in her jaws and jumped up on top of the fence carrying the eighty pound dog. The kittens all jumped over the fence and headed into the woods. The back door of the house opened again and there was a loud noise. The bullet hit the fence at her feet causing her to jump to the ground. She moved as fast as she could, dragging the dog.

The dog's intestines trailed on the ground and she kept stepping on them until they tore away from the opened chest cavity. Jake ran to the side gate, opened it and ran around to the back where the cougar had jumped off the fence. Holding the 9mm pistol extended in front of him, he searched in the darkness. It wasn't there, so he went into the woods a short distance, looking around. He was upset, the cougar had his dog. Then he realized that being out there in the dark with a cougar might not be a good idea. A chill went down his spine and the hair on the back of his neck bristled, standing straight up. He began backing up out of the woods.

Returning to the house, he picked up the phone and dialed 9-1-1. Fifteen minutes later two county sheriff's cars pulled up in front of the house. Jake met the officers at the street, leaving his pistol in the house, and told them what happened. They walked around the back of the house and the deputies shined their flashlights around looking for any evidence of a cougar. There was some blood on the ground, but not much. They found the drag marks, then the intestines, stretched out on the ground. The drag marks soon disappeared when the forest floor became covered with leaves. They looked around for over an hour without finding the culprit.

"I've never heard of a cougar around here before. This housing development is surrounded by woods so I guess it's not out of the question," one of the deputies said. "I know they can be hard to find, especially in the dark. Without tracking dogs, it's pretty much impossible, we'd only find them if they wanted to be found. Even if we had tracking dogs there's no guarantee of finding it. I'm sorry about your dog sir. We'll bring some trackers out here tomorrow and see if they can get the scent."

The deputies pulled away a little after midnight and stopped at a fast food place to get some coffee and make out a report.

"Kind of odd that a cougar might be in the housing area," one said. "Maybe the homeowner was mistaken?"

The other replied, "The story was consistent with the evidence. Bullet hole in the fence, blood, intestines and what looked like it could be drag marks."

"True, guess we'll have to see what happens with the dogs tomorrow."

Swawa heard the man follow them into the woods. She carried the dead dog until they were about a half a mile away from the housing area. Because of the gunshot and the man following them she used a different tactic for feeding on the dog. She laid the dog down and they took turns feeding, one at a time. The others hid out under the cover of some bushes. Each one fed for about one minute, then left and another came in to feed. After the dog was completely consumed Swawa decided that the housing area presented too much danger and it was not providing enough food for the four of them to survive.

She took the kittens and headed east, back into the deep woods. They traveled periodically during the day and night, taking breaks to sleep for three to four hours at a time. Three days later they were able to kill a deer that provided food for all of them for two days. A few days later they were all lying in a tree sleeping in the afternoon when a deer walked beneath them. One of the kittens heard it and dropped out of the tree, landing on its back. The noise woke the others and they quickly finished the job. This seemed to Swawa like a good place to stay for awhile.

Photo by Lee Dygert

7

Monday morning during breakfast Buck said to Eric, "I talked to grandpa yesterday about you going cougar hunting. He suggested we go to the reservation and talk with someone there who might have some experience. I'm picking him up this morning and we're meeting an old friend of his for lunch today at the reservation." To Marie he said, "I'll probably have dinner with dad too so I may be late getting home."

"That's okay" Marie said, "I'll bring home pizza, everyone will be happy, me included."

"Sounds good," the kids said as they gathered their things for school.

"See you later dad," Eric added.

Wendy gave Buck a hug, "Say 'hi' to grandpa for me. Love you."

"Bye dad," Bob said as they all headed for the door.

"Enjoy your day with your dad." Marie said as she gave him another hug and grabbed a cup of coffee for the way to work.

They arrived at the reservation at eleven where Mary owned a small trading post. "Hi Jack" as she gave him a hug. "This must be Buck. It's been years since I saw you." Giving him a big hug also, she announced "I've got a small lunch menu here. By the way lunch is on me."

"Well that's mighty nice of you. I was planning on taking you to lunch though," Jack responded.

"Thanks, but White Cloud and I have already made some sandwiches and there's clam chowder ready for the lunch crowd."

As a husky man with jet black hair came out of the kitchen, Mary introduced him, "This is White Cloud."

They all shook hands, "It's been a long time," both Buck and Jack said.

They talked over old times as they ate lunch. Soon the conversation turned to cougar hunting.

"My grandson, Buck's son, has decided he's going cougar hunting. We were wondering if you might know someone here on the reservation who has some experience?"

"A friend I hunt deer and elk with sometimes has had some experience with cougars. In fact we were just talking about going hunting again last night. There he is now," White Cloud responded as a middle aged, slightly graying man came through the door.

White Cloud waved the man over and introduced them. "Soaring Eagle, this is Jack and Buck."

"Nice to meet you." After they all shook hands Soaring Eagle grabbed a chair and pulled it up to the table.

Looking directly at Soaring Eagle, Buck started the conversation. "My son seems to be intent on going cougar hunting and White Cloud says you might have some knowledge about it."

Soaring Eagle shook his head. "I haven't actually gone cougar hunting, but I have run into a few of them while deer hunting. Most of my encounters were in the last few years. There are ways to hunt them without dogs, but it is usually only by chance that you find them."

"I've thought about going cougar hunting off and on over the years, but the time just didn't seem right. I think it's time. I've got a score to settle. What do you think Soaring Eagle?"

"Sure sounds good to me. I love to hunt."

"Would you mind if we join you?" White Cloud asked.

"That would be great," Buck responded.

At breakfast the next day Buck said to Eric, "Grandpa and I went over to the Indian reservation yesterday to visit Mary, an old friend of his. Her husband, Two Hawks, was a friend of grandpa's many years ago. When grandpa found out you wanted to go cougar hunting he called her and they arranged for us to meet for lunch. Two Hawks was killed by a cougar at a logging camp about thirty-five years ago. His son, White Cloud, and I were friends as children. He has a lot of hunting experience, and he and his friend, Soaring Eagle, would like to join us cougar hunting. I think it would be better to go with someone who has some current hunting experience. What do you think?"

"Sure," Eric responded enthusiastically, "I like that idea."

"I thought you would, so I already set it up."

Wednesday after school Buck and Eric went to the sporting goods store to get the ammunition, freeze dried food packets, plenty of water purification tablets and whatever else they saw that looked like they might need.

Buck asked the sales associate, "Do you know anything about cougar hunting?"

"I'm a deer hunter, I've never hunted cougar myself, but I get a cougar hunter in here occasionally," the associate responded.

"Do they have any luck without dogs?"

"Oh yeah, they usually have pictures with them when they come in, and they're always eager to show them to me."

"How do they find them?"

"From what they tell me there's three methods that work well. The first is the predator call, a wounded elk, distressed new calf, or fawn. The second method is using a wild turkey call. The wild turkey population is growing like crazy and the cougars have developed a taste for them. Using a blind is usually best for those two methods. The other method is a little unusual. It takes two hunters, the first leaves alone down a predetermined path to a specific destination. The second hunter follows fifteen minutes later to get the cougar that's following the first.

"Now that doesn't sound like much fun."

"From what the hunters tell me the method works, sometimes."

"OK, we'll take a predator call, a turkey call and a blind big enough for two."

On the way home Buck asked, "Do you want to be the decoy or the follower?"

"I think I'll try the calls. It sounds like a lot more fun."

Thursday after school Buck and Eric went out to the garage and got their backpacks down from the overhead. In the family room they began to lay out all the items they would need for their hunting trip. They started with clothes; heavy socks, long underwear, and fleece tops. Everything went on the floor in sequential order, dark colored ski hat with shirts on top then pants. Then the socks on bottom so they could tell how many sets they had. They planned for a three-day trip, but figured it could be extended to five if necessary. They set out the freeze dried packets of food, two water containers each, water purification tablets, ramen, rice and individual flavored oatmeal packets. Other supplies were the rifles, a gun cleaning kit, ammunition, hunting knife, fire starting sticks for wet weather, tent, cold weather sleeping bags and lightweight, auto-inflate ground pads. When they were satisfied they had everything they needed they loaded the packs and weighed them. They tipped the scales at just over forty pounds each.

"Hey, we could fly up there to the meadow again." Eric said. "Maybe the plane would bring that cougar back."

"As an emergency landing it worked, but I don't think I would plan a flight in there. Besides, you have to think about the weight and balance limitations. We'd probably be okay with a four seat plane going in there.   Our extra equipment would be like two passengers in the back seats. If we get a cougar, where would we put it? Plus we'd have all that extra weight. I'd rather take off from a field like that underweight. Always stack the deck in your favor when you're flying."

"I didn't think about the extra weight. I guess driving is a better idea. How long will it take to get there?"

"Let's take a look at the map and see." Buck got the Washington map out and they studied it to find the right place. "This is basically where we're going. I picked up a detailed map of the area at the forest service yesterday. It shows an old logging road most of the way to the meadow, right here. It looks like about two miles to hike in from where the map shows the road ending. However, these forest maps are not always totally accurate about the roads. We're meeting White Cloud and Soaring Eagle at the small cafe in Arlington tomorrow morning at six. We'll have them follow us up there."

At five in the morning their alarm clocks sounded off. Buck got up, dressed and went to check on Eric. He was sleepily trying to put his feet on the floor. "Good morning Eric, ready to go? We're meeting White Cloud and Soaring Eagle at the small cafe at six."

"I'm working on it. Be there in a few minutes."

"Okay let's get going." Buck went back to his bedroom and kissed Marie good bye.

"Be careful," Marie said softly, and watched as he walked out the bedroom.

By the time Eric made it to the living room Buck had poured two cups of coffee.

"Stay up too late last night?"

"About midnight. No coffee for me."

"That's pretty late, could be a long day for you."

"Nah, I'll sleep while you drive, at least to the café anyway."

They pulled into the parking lot at the small café as White Cloud and Soaring Eagle were getting out of the truck.

"Good morning," Buck and Eric said as they got out of the SUV.

"Morning," they both said, shaking hands and heading for the café. "It's a nice day," White Cloud observed looking up at the sky. "I hope the weather is this nice up in the mountains for our hike in to the campsite area.

"Would be nice, I'm sure it will be a little cooler, let's hope it isn't raining."

Inside they sat at a large booth and all ordered coffee, except for Eric who ordered hot chocolate, and big breakfasts, not knowing when they would eat next. All of their food for the next few days was either dry or freeze-dried. This would be their last regular meal for a few days. Eric had two orders of hash browns, eggs and sausage.

Buck pulled the two maps out of his jacket pocket and laid the state map out first. "Here's the general area, we'll take highway two from here to this area." He spread out the forest map next.

"From there we'll take this logging road to here," showing the end of the road and a probable parking area. "From there we hike into the meadow. I imagine there'll be some kind of trail. If not, we may have to use the compass and make our way there."

"Looks like you've planned it out very well," White Cloud said. "Soaring Eagle and I have been studying the maps too and we pretty much came up with the same plan.

At six forty-five everyone was finished eating and Buck asked, "Shall we head up the mountain?"

They all nodded and got up, paying their bills on the way out.

"You've been studying the maps of the area Buck, we'll follow you," White Cloud said on the way to their vehicles.

They drove up the mountain on the two-lane highway. The river paralleled the road along the south side of the car. "Looks like some good fishing holes down there," Eric observed. "Maybe we ought to come back and try them out sometime."

"Yes, it's a nice looking river. Have to find out when the salmon are here. Not likely there'll be any trout in a river on the east side of the Cascades."

"Why not?"

"Salmon are big business in Washington. Trout love salmon eggs, so there's hardly any trout in western Washington rivers that have salmon runs."

"Guess that makes sense, but it's a bummer, because the salmon are only in the river for a few weeks a year."

"That's why we go to the lakes for trout. Some of the lakes are planted with thousands of trout every year, mostly Rainbows, but also Cutthroat, Dolly Varden and browns."

"Do you think we'll get a cougar?"

"Don't know, but it should be a nice campout if it stays dry."

They passed the tiny town indicated on the map, if one could call it a town. It consisted of four houses and a decaying, long since deserted country store. Buck checked the odometer, the map indicated two point five miles to the logging road. At two point three miles he slowed down and saw the forest service logging road sign up ahead. He checked the rear view mirror, and White Cloud had turned on his signal indicator too. He pulled off the main highway onto the dirt road and within two miles switched the SUV into four wheel drive. Thirty minutes later the road was a mass of ruts, water run off ravines and too much foliage growing in the road. When they could go no further they found a wide area in the rut and stopped the trucks.

They all got out and looked around. "Looks like this is the end of the road," Buck observed.

"Yep, might as well get our gear and pack in from here," White Cloud replied, and they all loaded up their packs, shouldering their rifles.

They started hiking due south. It was no longer a road, but was passable as a trail.

On the hike into the planned campsite Buck said, "We were at the sporting goods store picking up supplies yesterday and the sales associate gave us some advice. He said to try predator calls and turkey calls. He also told us about a hunter leaving on a trail and then a follower about fifteen minutes later to catch the cougar following the first hunter. Ever heard of that method?"

"Yes, in fact that's the method Soaring Eagle and I were planning to use"

"Sounds a little bizarre to me," Eric said.

"We spoke to an elder of the tribe who did some cougar hunting in his younger days," White Cloud said. "It was his recommended method. It's not uncommon for cougars to follow people in the woods. They're mostly just curious, and the people hardly ever know they're being followed. In some of the cases where people have been attacked the authorities tracked the animal and found the cougar had been following the victim for a mile or more. In some cases it was just waiting for a person to be alone. There's been a few children attacked, some killed, when they got ahead of the group of people they were with, out of their sight. The cat was just holding off until it had opportunity where it could take a single individual and disappear without a trace of evidence."

"Won't that be what you're doing by using the decoy method, giving it an opportunity?"

"Sort of, it's a calculated risk. We both hunt alone on a regular basis so it's not like it's really that different," Soaring Eagle said. "I've had a cougar follow me when I've been hunting before. Probably lots of times, but I've only actually seen them five or six times."

"Did you shoot them?" Eric asked with curiosity.

"No, but I don't particularly like them following me if I know they're there, especially when I'm alone. Virtually every attack that has occurred in the last fifteen years was on a person that was alone. When they allow you to see them, it means they have shifted into a more aggressive mode. I usually shoot a couple rounds near their feet to scare them off. It's only a temporary retreat though. Cougars are never afraid of people, even with a gun. I think they're really smart animals. I think that they can see the rifle and it should be a deterrent, but it isn't from my experience. It's just instinct to follow something that's moving."

"I was deer hunting about ten years ago and came across a young one playing with a snowball," White Cloud injected. "It didn't know I was there so I watched it for about a half hour. It just kept batting the snowball around, like a housecat playing with a ball of string, pretty awesome experience really."

"So why didn't you shoot it?" asked Eric.

"Didn't see any reason to. It was a young one, and we weren't having problems with them then, like we are now."

"Do you think we'll find any on this trip?" Buck asked.

"You never know when you're going to run into one," Soaring Eagle said. "The predator calls will substantially increase the chances though."

"Are you going to try the predator calls too?" Eric questioned.

"That will be part of the plan. Soaring Eagle will lead the way to an area we have predetermined, and I will follow him. If we don't attract one on the way to our destination, we'll sit down in a good spot and start calling."

"How about you two, what's your plan?"

"We've got a blind. We're going to find a good spot and use the predator calls. Do you have any suggestions?" Buck asked.

"It might be a good idea to have something directly behind you, like a cliff or big tree. Makes it harder for them to sneak up on you from the back and catch you by surprise," Soaring Eagle replied.

"You probably want a place where you can see a few hundred yards if possible. The farther out you can see them the better. That way you can watch it as it comes in. Twenty to one hundred yards would probably be a good distance for a shot."

"That's good advice, thanks," Buck said.

They arrived at the edge of the big meadow at noon. Within ten minutes, they found a flat area for the tents under some big maple trees, and conveniently right next to a stream. It was a good place to watch the meadow in the evening and early morning and the stream had good, clear, running water.

"This looks like an ideal place," White Cloud observed.

"Yes, it has everything we need," Soaring Eagle added.

"Looks good to me too," Buck said. "Let's set up camp."

"I'm ready to get this pack off. It's starting to get heavy," Eric groaned as he removed his pack.

Soaring Eagle looked at Eric, "You're a young man, this should be an easy stroll for you."

"Yeah, well I stayed up a little too late last night."

Both of the tents were the quick erect, dome style. Buck and Eric were in one and White Cloud and Soaring Eagle in the other. When the tents were up, they laid out their sleeping pads and bags.

"Let's get some rocks from the stream and make a fire pit now so we don't have to do it later," White Cloud recommended.

"Sure, I'll go to the stream and toss some up here," Eric volunteered.

Soaring Eagle gathered wood for the fire while the others set up the fire pit.

Around one-thirty the campsite was ready for the night.

"Shall we wander around and see what there is to see?" Buck suggested.

"Sounds good to me," White Cloud said. "We'll take the east side of the meadow if you would like to take the west side. It'll be getting dark between five and six. The sun sometimes sets fast in the mountains. Since we're in an unfamiliar area, we should plan to be back here well before dark."

They all sat on logs around the fire pit, loading their rifles. "That gives us a couple hours to look around," Buck looked at Eric, "are you ready?"

"Yep."

They walked side by side with their rifles slung over their shoulders. On the way to the center of the field Buck took out his compass. Looking around he found a mountain peak to the south and took a bearing line. Then he looked around again until he found another high point, a mountain range with an obvious bare spot, farther off to the east. He took another bearing line, making a mental note of the bearing and position of the meadow.

"It's one nine zero to the peak on the south range and one hundred degrees to that bare spot to the east," Buck told Eric. "Just in case we loose our bearing while we're here it may help us find our way back."

"Good idea, getting lost doesn't sound like much fun," Eric responded, memorizing the one nine zero and one hundred degrees.

They walked over to the edge of the meadow and a short distance into the surrounding woods. They soon came across a game trail. It was wide enough for them to walk, single file, without touching the growth on either side of the trail.

"This trail has to be frequently used by larger animals, like deer or elk," Buck indicated. "Yep, here's some deer droppings," he pointed out to Eric. "They're fairly fresh too, less than a day old for sure."

"Here's some good deer prints in the powdery dirt," Eric noted.

Buck took a look, "Sure is, this one's a buck. See the way the two hoof prints are parallel. This one over here is a doe. Look at the way the leading edge of the print comes together, a little like an upside down 'v' with an open end. They're both fairly big one's too."

Following the path, Buck kept looking up the trail then down to the ground for prints. "We really need to find some mud, makes for better prints."

"Mud means rain, we don't need any of that."

"Old mud that has dried out is okay too. It can hold a print for days sometimes."

About thirty minutes before the sun would touch the horizon Buck said, "We haven't found any cougar prints yet, or anything else that would indicate a lion presence. If we could find a covered cougar kill, that would be a good place to stake out. Probably be just dumb luck if that happened. I think it's time to head back to camp."

They followed the trail back until they could see the edge of the meadow. Taking a side trail they walked out into the south end of the clearing and through the meadow back toward their campsite. Along the way they noticed a deer beginning to forage at the edge of the meadow. Just before they reached the northern side of the meadow near their camp a big nine point bull elk walked out of the woods. It was less than fifty yards from them.

"Whoa look at that," Eric said in amazement. "It's huge."

It looked over at them as it continued to head out farther in search of greener grass.

"Doesn't seem to care much about us being here, does it," Buck observed.

"Too bad it isn't elk season, that's a nice one."

"Deer and elk seem to know when they are in season. They disappear until the season is over. Must be something they pass down through the generations. The first rifle shot and they're gone. All of the deer and elk can see that we're carrying rifles, but it doesn't seem to matter to them right now."

They propped their rifles up against a tree when they arrived at the campsite. "If you can get the fire pit going Eric, I'll get some water to boil."

Eric gathered some kindling and lit the small pinecones at the base. Within minutes he had a small fire well under way and he added some bigger pieces. While he was gathering some more deadwood White Cloud and Soaring Eagle walked out into the edge of the meadow about one hundred yards away, waving at them.

Buck had two pots of water propped over the fire by the time they reached the campsite.

"Have any luck?" Eric asked.

"No, just getting familiar with the area. We found the trail on the map that looks like a good way to go for our plan. I figure we'll go out for about two hours until White Cloud stops and waits for me to catch up, or get the cougar following him. How about you two, see anything interesting?"

"No, not really, just scouting out the area. We'll probably head out that way again until we find a good spot to set up the blind," Buck said.

They sat with their backs to a log near the fire and watched the bull elk while the water heated for the freeze-dried chicken dinners.

"I wonder how old that bull is?" Eric asked.

"They shed their antlers every year. Generally, they add a tine for each year. With nine spikes he's probably about nine years old," White Cloud said.

"How much do you think he weighs?" Eric asked.

"That one probably weighs between eight and nine hundred pounds. I've shot bigger ones, they can weigh over a thousand pounds."

"That's a lot of meat to haul out. It could take days if you had to go very far," Eric said with amazement.

"It definitely is a job. Some of that weight is in the hide, sometimes sixty to eighty pounds fresh off the animal. The head and bones will weigh another hundred pounds, the intestines and internal organs can weigh up to a hundred pounds. Usually we carry out the legs with the bone. Most of the other meat is sliced off."

"Do you get all the meat that way?"

"Not all of it. Butchering an animal out here in the woods is not like having it in a butcher shop. Since it's usually pretty cold, and may even be frozen by the time you've made four or five trips. Some of it gets left, but nothing goes to waste in the woods. Whatever remains will provide food for raccoons and many other animals of the forest for days. Since most deer and elk hunting is done in the winter the remains will stay fresh for weeks. Winter is a time when it is hard for the animals to find food, what we leave actually helps the other animals to survive through the winter," Soaring Eagle said.

"I've had elk meat at Jeremiah's before, it's really good. I like it better than beef."

"Speaking of food," White Cloud said, "I'm getting hungry."

They all agreed it was time to eat.

Buck handed Eric a meal pack and poured some hot water into his meal kit. White cloud and Soaring Eagle took out elk jerky strips and poured hot water into cups with dried potato flakes. They all sat quietly near the campfire, Buck and Eric on small, aluminum tripod camp chairs with a nylon seat about six inches wide on each side, weighing less than a pound each. White Cloud and Soaring Eagle sat on the logs around the campfire. When they finished their dinners they got a pan of water and washed their eating utensils. It was nearly eight when everything was put away.

"Time for some dessert," Eric announced. They were all sitting by the fire again. "I've got granola bars and chocolate bars," offering a choice to each.

"Nice choice Eric," White Cloud said, "thanks," taking a granola bar, as did Buck and Soaring Eagle.

They finished their snacks and White Cloud wisely said, "Time to string the food up into a tree before it gets too late."

"Good idea," Buck said, "you never know if there's bear around, but you always have to assume there is."

They placed all their food items into a bag that White Cloud provided, tied it shut and put a rope around the neck of the bag. Soaring Eagle tied a rock to the other end of the rope and threw it over a branch about twenty feet off the ground.

"OK," White Cloud said.

Soaring Eagle pulled the bag high into the tree and away from the tree trunk. When he felt it was high enough he tied off the end of the rope to another tree to hold it up there for the night.

"What time do you think we should get up tomorrow?" Buck queried.

"It'll start getting light around six-thirty. If we're up around five-thirty we should have time to eat and be on our way by first light," Soaring Eagle said. "We shouldn't try to travel in the dark here because we're not familiar with the area yet."

Around nine they agreed it was time to hit the sack. White Cloud got some water from the stream and doused the fire out. They all said 'good night' after taking one last leak in the woods first.

"I'm bushed," said Eric after he crawled into his sleeping bag.

"I'm a little tired myself," Buck added. "Sleep well."

Both were sound asleep in minutes, Buck snoring loud enough to draw curious attention.

Snap, the sound woke Buck. At first he wasn't sure if what woke him up was real or a dream. Peering in the darkness at his watch he pressed the button to illuminate the face, it was two-thirty. He felt a slight urge to relieve his bladder, that's probably what woke him up. He started unzipping his bag when he heard it again. A twig breaking and leaves being stepped on, close to the tent. He lay there unmoving, listening, for what seemed like an hour. Whatever it was out there that would make a twig break was probably not a small animal. Eventually, when there were no more sounds, he decided he didn't really need to go that bad and got comfortable again. The night sounds of the forest were as expected and he soon fell back to sleep.

Photo by Lee Dygert

8

White Cloud untied the rope and silently lowered the bag of food from the tree, taking it over to the log next to the dead campfire. Seemingly in unison the 'beep, beep' of watch alarms pierced the silence of the crisp morning air. Getting ready to start breakfast he turned up the light on the propane lamp. A pot of water was already on a propane burner and near the boiling point. Carefully, he poured the hot water over the coffee grounds to drip into the pot.

"Boy, that smells great," Soaring Eagle said coming out of his tent. He wore a buckskin shirt under a brown, wool lined elk hide jacket, denim pants and brown leather boots, the same as White Cloud.

"I'll second that," Buck said as he and Eric soon emerged from their tent. Both wore insulated light green camouflage nylon jackets with matching coveralls, and waterproof, insulated, lightweight, nylon shell hiking boots, not as rugged as leather boots, but lighter and much warmer.

"You got a head start on us," Buck said as White Cloud filled his cup, "but I'm glad you did. Thanks for the coffee, it's just what the doctor ordered."

"I've got a built-in alarm clock," White Cloud chuckled. "I'm almost always awake before it's time to get up.

"I'm usually up before the clock goes off too," Buck added, "guess I was really tired last night."

"Being out in the fresh air will sometimes do that to you," Soaring Eagle observed.

Foregoing the coffee, Eric took an oatmeal packet from the bag, poured it into a cup, added some hot water and stirred it up. "Um, this smells good too," eagerly spooning it down.

They all had some type of instant breakfast, then cleaned up the dishes. The birds began to sing as the light tried to peek through the tops of the trees.

Hunting in the northwest can be full of surprises. The weather can change in a short amount of time. More importantly, the forest density in some areas can cause people to loose their sense of direction. If a person gets lost, they'd better be prepared for a cold night. They each stuffed their sleeping bags back into their compact storage bag and put them inside their backpacks. They added the things that seemed important for the day, a six by six tarp, two bottles of water, water purification tablets, a box of shells, granola bars, trail mix, a pack of freeze dried food, meal kit, a whistle, water proof matches and a butane lighter, and a ski type cap. Eric strapped the blind to the back of his backpack. They checked their rifles and loaded them. Buck and White Cloud strapped hunting knives to their belts, while Soaring Eagle inserted a clip into his Smith & Wesson 9mm pistol and put it in his shoulder holster. Eric clipped a folding, stainless steel knife to the inside of his front right pocket. The knife had a small knob on the side of the blade so that it could be opened with one hand, automatically locking in place.

"We'll see you tonight," White Cloud stated.

Buck handed White Cloud a two-way radio. "Would you like to take this with you? It's good for about two miles, substantially more if the conditions are good. Eric and I both have one. The batteries are good for hours, but I recommend you don't use it unless there's a good reason. Like there's an emergency or some kind of problem. It's really simple to operate." Buck showed them how it worked. They all turned on their radios and did a radio check.

"I'd recommend you keep it off all the time until evening, if you're not going to make it back before dark. One hour before dark turn it on at the top of the hour for five minutes. We'll have ours on too. If there's some kind of problem before that, or you get a cougar, fire three shots in close succession and we'll turn on our radio."

"Sure, I've heard about these, but I've never seen one. This is a good idea."

Satisfied they were ready to go they lifted their backpacks and adjusted them, snapping the waist belt to keep the packs from shifting while they walked.

"I guess we're ready," Buck said looking at Eric and then White Cloud.

"Looks like we're ready too," Soaring Eagle said.

Soaring Eagle shouldered his rifle, "I'm on my way, see you in a few hours at the weeping tree." Looking at the others, "I'll see you guys tonight," and headed off.

"Guess we're on our way too," Buck said, and they headed off to the south.

"It's a tad cool this morning," Eric noted, putting on a pair of thin gloves. "Good thing we came prepared."

"Probably in the high thirties," Buck added putting on his gloves also.

They took the same trail as last night, watching the ground for tracks. There was an abundance of side trails, some big enough for a deer or elk, others obviously were used by smaller animals. In about an hour they came to a unique side trail. The opening going through the bushes was about four feet high and three feet wide, and nearly circular. It was almost like a tunnel going well back into the dense growth.

Eric was in the lead at the time and he stopped, studying the unusual trail.

"Will you look at this, it's really weird."

"Know what made it?" Buck asked.

"No clue."

"Think about it, what's that size."

"Well you obviously know. I didn't get to go hunting all the time when I was growing up like you did."

"It's a bear trail."

Eric looked around, then at the ground.

"I don't see any bear tracks."

"Ground's too hard here. We'll probably find some sooner or later. Bears make their own way to the main trails, similar to the smaller openings we saw merging with the main trail. They have their own space. If we could follow the bear trail far enough we'd probably find its sleeping place, up in a tree most likely, but maybe a hollowed out tree trunk or a big fallen tree. They migrate some, but not as much as a cougar.

"What if we run into it?"

"Well we've got bear tags too, so I guess we can take a bear if we want. The meat is pretty good. Dad brought home a few when I was a kid. The loggers didn't like them hanging around the logging camp. They have a well developed sense of smell. The cook making the evening meal would send out plenty of delectable odors to draw them in. After dark they'd come into the camp area looking for scraps. If they didn't find anything to eat they'd raid the cook tent, which was always full of food and it was hard to keep that much food secure from the bears. Back then things were different, no one gave a second thought to shooting a bear under those circumstances. The cook would butcher it for dinner the next day and salt down what was left to keep for later meals, or make jerky out of it. In fact, anytime they saw a bear around the logging operation, they'd shoot it."

"Yeah, well I'm not sure I'd like a bear hanging around where I was working either."

"They can be dangerous if you get between them and food, during mating season, if it's a mother with cubs, or if it's just in a bad mood. Mostly though, they just want you to go away. They don't like people in their territory. I've run into them when I was backpacking quite a few times. I've never felt threatened at all. Maybe I was just lucky, those bears were used to people though, being around the backpackers. I've even been around a mother with cubs, she knew we were there. It's quite an experience to watch them, from a distance. You don't want to surprise one up close though, that would turn into a real problem in a hurry. I haven't ever run into one in an area where people are not common. Like out here where we are now, I doubt that there are ever any backpackers or other people around here very often. "

"You don't seem too concerned about them. I've always thought they were more dangerous than cougars."

"I don't think the statistics would support that. To my knowledge there's only been a few bear attacks on humans in the continental United States in the last fifteen years. There's been over sixty cougar attacks, thirteen of them resulted in death. Twenty of the others had permanent, incapacitating lifelong disabilities. The most common being the loss of one or both eyes and brain damage."

Buck took the lead as they departed from the bear tunnel. Taking his rifle off his shoulder he cradled it in the crook of his right arm. Eric put his rifle back on his shoulder as he traded places with Buck.

"What are we looking for?"

"Not sure, I haven't seen anything that looks like a good spot yet. How long has it been since we left the campsite?"

Eric checked his watch, "A little less than two hours."

Buck looked at his compass. They were still heading south. There was a clearing ahead of them.

"Let's go check that area out."

They saw a big tree butted against an embankment with a small grassy area.

"What do you think?"

"Yeah, that looks like a good spot." Eric took off his pack and laid it on the ground. "Right over there under that tree. It's a little elevated. We can see the whole open area. It's longer than the length of a football field, but that spot has the best visibility of the whole area."

"Let's set up the blind under that big tree," pointing at a large maple tree.

Eric carried his backpack over to the area and untied the blind. It was level ground and it only took them about fifteen minutes for it to be set up and ready for use. They put their packs up against the back of the enclosure on the tree side and propped their rifles up in the corner, one on each side. They opened their little tripod stools and sat down close to the front so they could easily see out the viewing slots. Eric took the wild turkey call and began calling.

Buck whispered, "Make the calls about five to ten seconds apart for awhile and we'll see what happens."

"The sun's getting higher and it's warming up a little," Eric whispered back.

"Yeah, maybe forty-five degrees. Probably get up to about fifty today, if we're lucky. But that's good if it stays cool. Cats are more likely to be active around midday if it's cool. On a warm day they may lay around in the shade most of the day."

About nine-thirty a covey of quail could be heard not far away. Before long the birds were running along the ground about thirty feet in front of them, two adults and ten to twelve babies. They dashed from one clump of wild blackberries to another, their top-knots waving back and forth. No sign of turkeys or big cats yet.

At eleven they opened their backpacks and took out some granola bars and trail snack.

"Pretty quiet so far, not that many animals out roaming around," Eric said.

"It's hard to tell what you'll run into when you're hunting an area that you're not familiar with. This is a potentially good area. Small grassy meadow, but it's a waiting game. We just have to sit and be patient."

Swawa and her kittens had spent the night roaming for prey without finding a single animal. It had been three days since they'd finished eating their last kill, a small deer of less than a hundred pounds. She found a good concealed area under a fir tree with low hanging branches and they all crawled in for a nap as the sun began to light the tree tops.

The kittens were more hungry than tired. Around nine all three decided to go back out to look for food. Two went together, but the other one took out on her own. The single cat went south, while the two walked north, single file, on a game trail until they came to an old logging road. The road gave them a greater field of view, but they continued to walk along the edge of the road next to the vegetation. It would provide them with a quick means of concealment if anything was sighted. After walking the road for about twenty minutes they saw movement coming toward them about four hundred yards away. Quickly they jumped off the road and into the brush. Hunkered down low to the ground they waited.

Soaring Eagle walked down the road whistling, 'I want to fly like an eagle'. He figured anything he could do that might help draw attention to him could help. Shuffling his feet to make a little extra noise, he passed the two cats, unaware of their presence. When he was about thirty yards up the road the cougars began following him, hugging the edge of the road.

After keeping their distance for twenty minutes Soaring Eagle came to a bend in the road. It curved to the left and began an incline up the side of a hill. The cats were familiar with the area. Instead of following him, they went up the side of the hill, crossed the road and jumped up onto a ledge above the road. They could hear him whistling as he drew nearer. Their muscles tensed, tails twitching. As he came into view they pressed down against the ledge, their concentration focused, muscles rippling the closer he got. As he passed beneath them they both noticed at the same time, movement on the lower road from where they had taken the shortcut. This new development took their full attention as Soaring Eagle whistled his way on up the road.

The cats relaxed and waited again. Ten minutes later they could see White Cloud in the distance approaching their position. They waited patiently as he slowly walked up the hill.

Soaring Eagle had taken another switch back and was getting a little tired from the long walk, especially the last twenty minutes up hill. He decided to stop for a short break. Standing at the side of the road, he looked over the edge. Below, he could see White Cloud walking up the road below him. He could also see the two cougars on the ledge above him. Quickly, he took the rifle off his shoulder, swinging it into position.

"Hey!" he yelled. Both cats turned to look uphill, but White Cloud didn't hear him and kept walking until he was out of sight to the right. Seeing Soaring Eagle standing there they bolted to his left just as he squeezed the trigger.

White Cloud yelled, "Hey, what's going on? Is that you Soaring Eagle?"

"It's me. There were two cougars on the ledge getting ready to jump you."

"Keep walking, I'll meet you at the bend." He started back down the road, staying at the edge, looking back to see if they would reappear.

When they met, White Cloud said, "Well, looks like the plan worked to some extent."

"Yeah, but there were two of them, that makes for a different story."

"How big were they?"

"They were both about the same size, but not full grown, eighty to a hundred pounds maybe."

"Young ones, odd they'd be together."

"Hard to tell, some places the females will stay between a hundred to one hundred twenty pounds most of their lives. They're still healthy, they're just not getting a lot to eat."

"That doesn't account for two of them being together."

"True."

"Let's go up to the place where you saw them and look around," White Cloud proposed.

"Good idea, at least we know there are cougars around. Doubt we'll find any prints in this hard ground, but it's a good place to start."

They walked back up the trail to where White Cloud was when he heard the shot.

"That's where they went," Soaring Eagle pointed out a place in the bushes.

"OK, let's go."

They left the road and went over the ledge on the down hill side. It was not steep, but rough walking through the smaller brush. When they arrived at the place where the two cougars disappeared they found a small game trail.

White Cloud took his rifle from the sling on his shoulder and held it with both hands. "You look downhill and I'll look around uphill." Soaring Eagle took out his Smith & Wesson 9mm and chambered a round, letting the hammer back down and then followed about fifteen feet behind him.

"You were right about the ground being too hard for prints. I'm not seeing any."

Twenty minutes later the game trail intercepted the road. The dirt became more powdery in the last twenty feet before the trail and road met. White Cloud crouched down.

"Good prints here." He laid his index finger down next to the prints, moving it around in a circular manner. "About four inches, nice and round, clear, crisp edges. Must be them, they're real fresh."

Soaring Eagle took a good look. "I concur, too many prints for just one cat."

They climbed up onto the road and looked around. "It's too compacted to tell which way they went," Soaring Eagle said.

"I've found that when they walk on a road they stay close to the edge of the road on the side that offers the most immediate cover. That way if something presents itself they can jump into hiding and wait," Soaring Eagle observed.

"That's good to know. You go down the road a little ways and I'll go up the road. See if you can find another trail, and look for prints."

Fifteen minutes later White Cloud yelled out, "Soaring Eagle, up here."

He was out of sight around a bend in the road, but not far away. When he arrived White Cloud pointed out two fairly good prints on the uphill side of the road.

"Looks like they stayed on the road, what's left of it. There's so much growing in it now it would be hard to drive, even with a 4x4. I think we're close to the end where we were going to meet."

"Let's head on up there. Maybe we'll get lucky. If we each got one on the first day, that would be pretty amazing."

"No kidding."

The two cougars were lying in an open space near the top of the hill soaking up the sun when they heard the men coming up the trail. They made off into the trees and found a clump of salal about thirty yards from the end of the trail. Flattening themselves down against the ground, they watched the clearing intently.

The top of the hill was well suited for logging operations. It was easily big enough for fifteen to twenty logging trucks to maneuver around, and relatively flat. Once out of the clearing the ground sloped off very gradually. One could see a good two hundred feet into the woods before the trees became too dense. The area had been logged and re-planted fifteen years before. The new evergreen trees were thirty to sixty feet tall with diameters ranging from six inches to twenty inches. It would be another fifteen to twenty years before they would be ready to be harvested again. The top of the hill had not been planted, but some smaller volunteer trees, salal, huckleberries, blueberries, blackberries and other types of indigenous plants had covered the area.

The cats watched from their position in the woods as White Cloud and Soaring Eagle sat down at the base of one of the larger trees, just outside of the clearing.

"I'll take this side of the tree, you take that side. That way they won't be able to sneak up behind us. There's a few game trails around," Soaring Eagle observed.

"Yeah, I saw some deer droppings a little bit ago. So there must be some animals using the area. The droppings were only a few days old. Shall we give it a try?"

"Go for it."

White Cloud retrieved the wooden device from his coat pocket. He took a look at it and wiped the mouth piece.

"Whoa," Waiting a few seconds before repeating, "whoa." The call was intended to imitate the sound of an elk calf in distress.

This immediately got the cougar's attention. Their ears perked up and they focused more keenly on the men. The cats were sure the sound was coming from the men. After twenty minutes of listening to the bogus elk calf the cats grew tired. Staying down with their bellies flat to the ground they curled their front paws under their chin and snoozed with one eye barely open.

"It's four o'clock, and it doesn't look like we're going to see any action. We'd better be heading back. It'll be dark before we get there as it is, but the road will be easy to follow," White Cloud said.

"Yep, we'd probably have better luck closer to dark. Maybe we'll see them again on the way back."

They slowly got up. "Well it was a nice rest anyway," White Cloud said.

When the men were out of sight the two cats got up to follow. They stayed back along the edge of the trail, keeping enough foliage between them and the men to stay out of sight.

White Cloud took his rifle off his shoulder as they approached the area where they had previously seen the cougars. "Just in case," he said, looking up the side of the hill to the area where the cats had disappeared.

When they reached the place where the men had seen the cougars before, the cats left the road and went down the steeper side of the hill to intercept them. They found a ledge above the road and waited. When the men appeared their muscles tensed slightly, studying them as they came closer.

The cats muscles rippled with tension as the men passed in front of them, continuing down the road. When they rounded the switchback and were out of sight the cougars jumped from the ledge to the road, crossed, and went straight downhill to intercept them again. This time they were much closer, crouched down behind a log. Once again the men passed. Two full grown men together was too risky for an attack. They watched as the men went down the road and around the next bend. Out of sight they lost interest and headed back for a nap at the place where they had left their mother.

At three thirty Buck said, "It's about time to head back to camp. We don't want to get lost in the woods trying to find our way back."

"Might as well, nothing's happening here."

When they made it to the south edge of the meadow it was just starting to get dark. There was a lone deer that they could see across the meadow.

"We won't have any trouble finding our way back from here. Let's stake out the area for awhile and see if anything happens," Buck said.

"Sounds cool, watching the deer is always fun anyway." Eric took out the turkey call and warbled a few times.

A big bull came out on the east side of the meadow about half way to the other end.

"Now that's a big elk," Eric said.

"Yeah, he's a beautiful animal. Probably the same one we saw last night."

"Hey, it's five o'clock. I don't see anyone at the campsite. Maybe we should call White Cloud."

"Good idea," replied Buck, getting out the radio.

Realizing it was almost dark and they were still quite a distance from the camp, White Cloud remembered the radio. As soon as he turned it on he heard.

"White Cloud this is Buck. Can you hear me?"

"Hi Buck, where are you?"

"We're at the south end of the meadow, watching a deer and making turkey calls. Where are you?"

"We're just about off the hill, near the base. Probably another thirty minutes before we'll be at the campsite."

"OK, it's getting too dark to see anything very well so we'll be heading back to the camp soon. We'll get the fire going and a lantern to help you find the way. See you there."

By the time Buck signed out Eric was already on his feet. They walked back to the camp area along the west edge of the meadow.

"He didn't say anything about getting a cougar so I assume they didn't. Do you think they saw any?" Eric asked.

"Don't know, guess we'll find out when they get to camp."

When they arrived at the site the first thing they did was take off their packs. "Boy, it's nice to get that pack off," Eric said. They propped their rifles up against a tree.

"If you can get the fire going I'll get the lantern lit," Buck said.

"Sure, no problem," and he went to work gathering some kindling for the fire.

"The light should help them find the camp a little easier."

"Probably a lot faster," Eric said. After the fire was going he filled two pots of water at the stream. He climbed up the small bank and put the pots over the fire hanging from a make shift tripod that held a stick across the fire pit.

"The water should be hot enough in about twenty minutes. Do you think we should go back to the same place again tomorrow?"

"I don't know. Let's see what White Cloud and Soaring Eagle have to say when they get back," Buck said.

"Hi guys," White Cloud said as they walked into the camping area.

"Wow, I had no idea you were there," Eric said. "How did you get so close without us hearing you?"

"It's sort of an Indian thing I guess," Soaring Eagle said. "We're taught to move around quietly in the woods from the time we're kids."

"How'd it go? Did you have any luck?" Buck asked.

"We actually saw two, I should say Soaring Eagle saw two."

"Where are they? Why didn't you bring them back?" Eric asked.

"Seeing them and being able to bring one back are not the same thing," Soaring Eagle lamented. "They were stalking White Cloud instead of me. Luckily I was looking over the ledge and saw them. So I guess the plan worked, just not the way we intended it to. I had to wait until he was clear to get a shot and they spooked just as I was firing. We looked around for them, even got some prints along the way, but we never did see them again. We should have gone directly after them instead of joining up first. Hindsight is always twenty-twenty."

"Maybe we should all go that way tomorrow," Eric responded.

"I think we'll have better luck working in pairs. With four grown men together we'd be less likely to have an encounter. They are very smart animals. They do a lot of observing before making an attack. However, since we know that there are two in that general area it wouldn't be a bad idea for you to go in roughly the same direction. Maybe circling the hill we went up today would be a good idea," Soaring Eagle suggested.

"Sounds like a good plan to me. Do you think we can still use the turkey calls while we're moving?" Buck asked.

"I think it would be best to find some cover, use the call for about thirty minutes and if nothing happens then move to a new spot and do the same. Probably walk about fifteen to thirty minutes before repeating the process," Soaring Eagle recommended.

"OK," Eric said. "I hope it works, at least we know there are two in the area. Which reminds me, I've been studying cougars and everything I've read says they're solitary. So why were there two together?"

"That kind of has us stumped too," said White Cloud.

"How big were they?" Eric wanted to know.

"That's another thing that has us wondering. They probably weighed between eighty and one hundred pounds," White Cloud answered.

"It's possible they were full grown, but not likely around here. This is real cougar country. They'd be much bigger if they were full grown. When they are living close to populated areas they tend to weigh about a hundred pounds all their adult lives. It's pretty much because they exist on dogs, cats and an occasional raccoon. It's enough for sustenance, but not as much to eat as a deer once a week, like they tend to do out here. In this area you'd expect an adult cat to weigh between one-thirty and two-twenty. The biggest one ever taken was in Hillsborough, Arizona in 1919. It weighed two hundred and seventy-five pounds," Soaring Eagle responded.

"Sounds like you've been doing your homework. So the question is still, why were there two together? They were probably too young to be a male and female during mating season. That's about the only time you see two together unless it's a mother with a kitten. Considering the size that doesn't seem likely either. Two cats hunting together could take about anything. We need to be extra careful and be a little more observant of the things around us," White Cloud said.

"That's probably a wise thing to do. When we were at the sporting goods store getting ammo and supplies there was a newspaper article pinned to the corkboard near the cash register. The clerk said a friend had sent it to him. A deer hunter in California, last season, was attacked while he was relieving himself, barely got his rifle in time. It was in the air coming at him when he shot it," Eric replied.

"That's a little too close," White Cloud said.

"What do you say we get some dinner going," Buck suggested.

"Good idea, I'm starving," Eric added.

They all got their meal kits and packets of freeze dried food. Soaring Eagle took the water pot off the stick above the fire pit and poured some onto each meal kit. As they sat around the fire eating dinner they heard the 'whoo whoo whoo' of an owl off in the distance. A few minutes later they could hear something moving through the limbs and leaves of the trees, almost a crashing sound not far away.

"What was that?" Eric wondered.

"It was probably an owl going after a squirrel or something else in a tree. They're usually pretty quiet in an attack, but sometimes they can make a lot of noise going through the leaves of a tree going after their prey. It's dark and usually the prey can't see as good as the owl," White Cloud said.

"What do they usually eat?" asked Eric.

"They eat mostly mice and rats, smaller animals, occasionally a squirrel or a rabbit, the animals that are active at night, which is most wild animals. It's all part of the food chain, except that the owls don't have many predators. They have very sharp talons. Once the animal is impaled they don't usually get away. With the bigger animals, a quick bite to the back of the neck finishes them off, their beaks are sharp and powerful."

By the time they finished eating and cleaning up the dishes it was close to eight-thirty. They all found a seat around the campfire and warmed their hands.

"My father, Two Hawks, was killed by a cougar when I was very young," White Cloud started. "Cougar attacks on humans were relatively rare back then, much like today. The attack scenario hasn't changed much though. They virtually always attack an adult when the person is alone. They're very smart animals, and I think they size up a situation to determine if they can make a successful attack without being hurt. That's why they stalk a potential victim for so long, passing up many opportunities, waiting for just the right time. They want to take the victim totally by surprise. If they think they have a good chance, they run ahead to a ledge, a tree over the path or some kind of cover, so they will only be a few feet from the victim when the person walks past. Most of the time the victim doesn't even know what hit them right away. A crushing bite to the back of the head of a child could render the child incapacitated in two or three seconds.

There's been three children killed by cougars in the past ten years that were hiking with a group of family and friends. All were boys, under ten years old, and all were in Colorado. The child ran ahead on the trail where the group could not see him, and the cat took the opportunity it had been waiting for. In two of the cases the child seemed to simply disappear. The cat was able to attack, render the child incapacitated and drag him away before anyone in the group realized he was gone. In the other case the cat was caught in the act and frightened away, but even the assistance of trained nurses in the hiking party could not save him.

Attacks on adults are usually different. They put up a fight and manage to persuade the cat that they are not food, unless the victim is seriously injured in the initial attack. When that happens, only the assistance of someone nearby can save them.

However, coming to someone's assistance can be a problem too. I've studied the attack scenario of three different cases where a woman was hiking with children when one of the children was attacked by a cougar. In each case there were no grown men in the group. The women all apparently launched a serious attack on the cat, trying to get it off the child. The cat then turned on the woman and killed her in each of the cases. As near as I can figure, if you grab a cougar that is attacking someone, or touch it with your arm or leg in any way it is much more likely to turn on the rescuer with a vicious attack. It is hard to keep away from the cougar in a situation where someone is being attacked, but the best method is to stand there yelling and screaming at it and waving your arms above the head. If that doesn't work throw stones at it. As a last resort poke it with a long stick until it gives up the attack."

"So what do we do if it happens to one of us?" Eric asked.

"We're in a different situation than those women were, they apparently were not carrying guns, which would be what you would probably expect in each of these incidents, a woman out for a walk in the woods with some children. If for some reason it happens to one of us, just shoot it. Try to hit it right in the front shoulder or along the back so it hits the spine and paralyzes it. If you don't have your gun stab it right between the shoulder blades as deep as you can or in the throat."

Photo by Lee Dygert

9

Buck was the first to emerge from the tent the next morning. "Rise and shine, it's five o'clock," he announced.

White Cloud opened their tent and said, "Morning Buck," Soaring Eagle was right behind him. Eric was starting the fire while Buck boiled some water for coffee and hot cereal.

"Morning," said Eric, "the fire's going well enough to keep us warm while we get some breakfast."

Soaring Eagle stood next to the fire warming his hands, "Feels good, is the coffee ready yet?"

Buck finished pouring the water over the grounds and poured out three cups, then put some hot chocolate mix in another cup and mixed in some water for Eric. Each gratefully took a cup and expressed their thanks.

By five thirty they had finished eating their hot cereal and about three cups of coffee each. Eric stopped at two cups of hot chocolate. It took them about ten minutes to clean up and get ready for the day of hunting. Shortly after six they all put on their backpacks, loaded with survival gear, slung their rifles over a shoulder and walked away from the campsite together. They headed east toward the area where White Cloud and Soaring Eagle had seen the cougars yesterday.

Initially they hiked four abreast along the edge of the meadow. The sky was beginning to light up, just enough for them to see where they were going.

"I recommend we split up again at the same place where we did yesterday and use the same method," White Cloud said to Soaring Eagle. "Buck and Eric, you might want to stay with me until we get to the base of the hill. From there I'll follow Soaring Eagle up the hill the same way we did yesterday and you two circle around the hill using your turkey calls."

"Sounds good to me," Eric responded.

When they reached the trail that left the meadow and lead to the old logging road they had to travel single file. White Cloud led the way.

At seven twenty they arrived at the split up point.

"See you later," Soaring Eagle bid to the others, as he continued on the trail.

"We might as well sit for a bit," White Cloud said, checking his watch. "We'll give him a fifteen minute head start. We should be to the hill by about eight thirty." They each found a good sized rock and took off their packs and rifles, leaning them against the rocks they sat down.

"How long do you think it will take us to make it all the way around the base of the hill?" Buck asked.

"I don't really know how long it will take to go the whole way around. I'd recommend you get a bearing on a couple of prominent features before you start and then take another bearing about noon. If you aren't sure you're half way around then I'd say it would be a good idea for you to return back the same way you went.

"I think that's a good idea. Things like this can be deceptive when you're in an area that you are not familiar with. Plus the time we take stopping to use the turkey call and waiting to see if a cougar shows up will add to the transit time," Buck added.

"It's been long enough, shall we head out," White Cloud suggested.

"Let's go," Eric and Buck both responded.

Near eight thirty White Cloud announced to Buck and Eric, "This is pretty much the base of the hill. There is a game trail over there off to the left," pointing as he explained. "You'll probably want to go about fifteen to thirty minutes then stop and use the turkey call. If nothing happens, then walk another fifteen to thirty minutes and try again. Find an area, like a meadow, that is clear enough for you to see all around the perimeter. Once in your hiding place you should be able to watch the game trails that lead into the clearing. Cougars almost always use established trails. There are two reasons for that, first is that it's easier walking than going through rough areas or brush. Secondly, it's quieter. Cougars are masters of the stealth approach.

Once you are concealed start using your turkey call. When or if the cougar comes in he's going to be quiet, trying to sneak up on the turkey. Keep an eye out for colors and shapes that don't quite fit in with what you are seeing. Most importantly, watch for movement. Generally they move slowly when tracking their prey. As it gets closer it will probably be crouching down, ready to spring, making it even harder to see it.

"Let's plan to meet right here at three-thirty. It may be dark by the time we get back to camp but I feel pretty comfortable we'll be able to find our way back now that we've been here three times. Good luck."

Buck took out his two way radio from his shirt pocket and said, "Shall we test the radios first."

"Good idea," White Cloud responded as he removed his jacket pocket.

Buck and Eric started walking toward the game trail and Buck keyed his radio, "White Cloud, this is Buck."

"Hi Buck, you're coming in good. Why don't we make a call at noon to check in again?"

"Okay," Buck keyed his radio as they continued toward the trail, leaving the clearing and going single file, Buck in the lead. "Sounds like a good plan. Talk to you at noon, out." Looking behind him they had already lost sight of White Cloud.

"Well Eric, looks like we're off on a new adventure."

"Hope we see one today Dad. That would be way cool. I'm ready to get one, I've been waiting for this for a long time."

"Yeah, the fact that we already know there's at least two around here increases our chances."

"Good thing you thought about removing the camouflage material from the blind frame and leaving the frame at our campsite. Just carrying the material makes it a lot lighter. Sounds like we'll be walking more today so I'm glad for the lighter pack, it will make it much easier for me."

"Yes, that's exactly what I figured too. It won't be as good as the whole blind, but it should work okay and we won't have to spend so much time putting it up and taking it down every half hour. Guess we're about to find out how well it works, there's a clearing up ahead."

As they emerged from the trail they could see that the open area was about 25 yards by 40 yards. There was eight to ten game trails around the perimeter.

"Here's a good vantage point," Eric said pointing to a group of huckleberry bushes about four feet high. The foliage was thin enough to see through, but broke up their silhouette.

"Ah, good pick, this will do just fine."

Eric got out the camouflage material and spread one piece on each side of their position, leaving the back and front completely open. They hid behind the berry bushes and Buck began to work the call.

After a couple of calls, Buck whispered, "Be ready. They can sometimes appear and disappear very quickly."

Nodding that he understood, and anxious to do something, Eric raised his rifle, chambered a round and put the safety on. He pointed the rifle out into the meadow, holding the barrel support with his left hand and resting it on his knee. Holding the stock with his right hand, he placed his index finger just outside the trigger housing. He slowly scanned the meadow from left to right and right to left, looking for movement or anything that had changed since his last scan.

The night before none of the cougars had been successful in finding prey once more. They returned to the same bedding area about five in the morning and quickly went to sleep. By eight, the three kittens were awake and hungry. The largest of the three went to the south alone, the other two headed to the east and stayed together to hunt for food. About nine, the larger kitten heard the distant gobble of a turkey. Once before they had killed a turkey, and she distinctly remembered the sound. The gobble reminded her that the last one proved to be a tasty meal.

Her need for food, and the sound of a potential meal encouraged her to move at a faster pace than she usually used while hunting. She was totally focused on pursuing the distant sound.

Disappointed, Eric quietly asked, "We might as well move on, we've been here for fifteen minutes now. If we stay in one place too long we'll never make it all the way around the hill today."

"True, maybe it doesn't really matter. This looks like a good place. Let's give it about five more minutes."

"Okay."

When the five minutes were up, just as Eric started to rise, he saw movement at the northwest end of the meadow. It was very slight but he knew it looked different than his last scan of the area. He focused on the spot and elbowed his Dad and whispered, "Look at the northwest end of the meadow, near the base of that big cedar tree. I think I saw something move."

Cautiously Buck reached for his binoculars and raised them slowly to his eyes. Holding his breath he peered into the binoculars. Letting his breath out slowly he whispered, "It's a cougar."

It inched forward just enough for Eric to get a good view. "I see it," with excitement in his voice.

With confidence, he slowly raised the rifle to his shoulder so the cat wouldn't detect any movement. He pressed the button to take the safety off, hoping it wouldn't hear the clicking sound it made and scare it away.

Buck quickly reminded Eric, "You need to account for the distance. Aim about one inch above where you want to hit it."

Now Eric had a good profile of the cat crouched down. It was inching its way forward and slowly turning its head from side to side, listening for the gobble.

Eric drew a bead on the cat, just off center, right and below the shoulder of its front leg. Slightly raising the rifle to compensate for the distance, he targeted the heart. Thinking to himself, 'what a magnificent animal,' and paused to absorb the beauty of his first cougar sighting. Deciding he'd better not take too long he pulled the trigger while Buck had the binoculars riveted on the cat.

"BANG!"

Eric glanced up, "I don't see it. Did I get it?"

The crouched cat felt the concussion of the bullet hit the tree only an inch above its shoulder blades and then heard the crack of the rifle.

"That's amazing. It just disappeared in the blink of an eye, as if it had never been there. The bullet hit the tree just above it's shoulder. Did you see the bark flying?"

"Wow, I actually saw one and got a shot at it. Cool! Think it'll come back?"

"That's hard to say, but my guess is we're better off going after it." Buck got out his radio, "White Cloud, this is Buck."

White Cloud already had his radio out when he heard the shot. "Was that you Buck?"

"Yeah, Eric got off a shot but missed it. You see anything yet?"

"All's quiet here. Talk to you later, good luck, out here."

Buck turned off his radio, "Let's go after it."

Anticipating his response, Eric was already folding the camouflage material and stuffing it into his backpack. They skirted the perimeter of the clearing until they got to the place where the cougar had disappeared down a game trail.

Eric led the way holding his rifle in front of him, safety on, ready for another chance. Buck chambered a round in his rifle, put his safety on and followed behind Eric about fifteen feet, keeping his rifle pointing off to the side of the trail.

Walking slowly Eric searched the bushes on both sides of the trail. Fifteen minutes later he began to relax, the lack of any action or activity eased his attentiveness. Quietly he asked his dad, "See anything yet?"

"No."

The two cougar sisters crouched down behind the bushes, well concealed, about fifty yards behind White Cloud. He stood at the edge of the old logging road looking up ahead for any sign of movement.

Creatures of habit, the cats had their hunting skills honed. They had watched this newest prey about the same time of the day yesterday. As White Cloud began walking they moved lower down the hill and began running along a narrow deer trail until they reached a bear tunnel. The tunnel ran through a clump of blackberry bushes that had grown, undisturbed to a height of over ten feet and covered a large area. The tunnel was about four feet high and nearly four feet wide. The cats could run through the tunnel without being seen and the ground was well worn, no twigs or branches that would make noise. The two sisters had run ahead of White Cloud and were waiting for his arrival.

White Cloud approached the place where Soaring Eagle had seen two cats the day before, his instinct told him to be cautious and ready. The information he had gathered over many years of studying cougar behavior told him they are repetitive in nature, so he figured the cats would be near the same location as yesterday. Knowing this valuable fact he chambered a round and left the safety off. He began to walk in the middle of the road instead of the edge of the high side as he did yesterday. He felt more exposed, but knew he would have a clearer view of the boulder from a distance. Unable to see anything yet he did notice that some branches were hanging over the boulder. As he passed in front of the boulder he still had not seen any sign of the cats, relaxing a bit, he lowered the rifle to his waist.

Soaring Eagle was sitting on a rock at the edge of the road, in the same place as he had the day before, when the reality of the situation suddenly hit him. The feeling was overwhelming that he should look at the downside of the hill, not just in front of him. Crossing over to the lower side of the road he looked down around the area finally focusing on the boulder. At first he didn't see anything, but the branches that covered part of the left side of the top of the boulder caught his attention. Then after watching for a few minutes he noticed movement and saw a tail moving. Shortly he saw a second tail moving between the branches. Quickly, and quietly as possible he chambered a round.

The two cats were crouched down low above the trail waiting for White Cloud to appear. This time the cats were nestled under the branches of a fir tree, one that lay on top of the east side of the boulder. As White Cloud appeared, about thirty yards down the road the cat's muscles rippled, their tails switching back and forth, faster and faster.

Soaring Eagle crouched down and inched his way sideways and a little closer to get a better angle. He had a clear view of the boulder and the road below it. He could see the tails moving, but the branches obstructed his view of the cats. He thought that it was better to wait and see what would happen in the next few minutes. Hopefully they would move so he could see a body outline better.

Within minutes White Cloud appeared to the left of the boulder, about ten yards away. Unable to see the cougars, Soaring Eagle's instinct focused on the tree branch just above the boulder. Within seconds the branches moved, but he could not see even an outline of either cat yet. Very slowly he removed the binoculars from the breast pocket of his buckskin hunting shirt. By the time he had them to his eyes, he could see White Cloud on the far side of the road passing in front of the boulder.

Focusing the binoculars on the tree branch he clearly saw the cougar's tail as it stretched out from the branches. He watched it as it began to twitch intensely and knew action was crucial. Almost instantaneously, he dropped the binoculars and raised his rifle as the cat jumped off the boulder.

Soaring Eagle yelled a quick warning, "Look out!"

White Cloud was on the low side of the road now looking up ahead, scanning the area when he heard the warning. It all happened just as he became aware of movement behind him. Instinctively he turned to his right and as he came around he raised his rifle into the port arms position. The cat was in the air less than a foot from him. He pushed the rifle forward meeting the cat and absorbed the blow which nearly knocked him off his feet. He pushed and turned to his left side knocking the cougar off in a glancing blow. The cat hit the ground on all fours and was ready for another attack. The tensing of White Cloud's muscles from the impact caused his index finger to slip off the trigger guard and a shot was fired into the air.

Soaring Eagle had fired a round into the side of the hill just as the cat pounced. He didn't dare try to shoot the cat since White Cloud was too close, it was intended to drive the cat away.

Surprised, the cat reacted to the two shots and bolted for cover. It managed to jump to the other side of the road in just one leap. White Cloud ran to the edge of the road, cocked his rifle and fired a round at the disappearing cat. It was moving so fast that it seemed to just vanish into the brush.

While the two men were focused on the attacker, the other cougar was still hidden under the branches on the boulder. Watching the events take place it quickly slipped into the underbrush and disappeared.

The attacking cougar didn't know what had happened but her keen instinct told her to get out of there. The potential for danger to her around hunters was not in her memory yet and she had no idea what made the loud sound, however she would remember this experience. After running for five minutes she spotted a smaller trail and decided to follow it. A huge spruce tree loomed up ahead and when she reached the base of it, she sprang in a single bound up twenty feet into the tree. Climbing another twenty feet up she found a branch large enough to hold her. After walking onto the limb, she looked at the ground and didn't see anything moving. Feeling safe and comfortable she turned around facing the tree trunk and lay down. Ten minutes passed as she watched the ground for activity. When nothing happened, her eyes grew heavy and she fell into a deep sleep.

Eric relaxed a little as time drew on and nothing had happened. He became less attentive about being quiet on the trail. Buck removed his clip and extracted the round from his rifle chamber. After he put the round back into the clip he snapped the chamber closed and replaced the clit.

"Looks like another opening up ahead," Eric noticed. "Let's give that one a try. We should be there pretty soon."

"Might as well. That's what we're here for. Let's stop a minute and call White Cloud, it's just now noon."

Suddenly they heard a shot, quickly followed by two more. "Maybe they got our cat?"

Buck keyed his radio, "White Cloud, it's Buck, over."

In the heat of the activity White Cloud had forgotten about his radio and it was still turned off. Going unanswered Buck said, "I think I'll leave the radio on for awhile. They might be too busy to realize that it's noon."

"Good idea," Eric started walking again.

Minutes later Buck's radio came to life, "Buck, it's White Cloud."

"Hey White Cloud, did you get a cougar?"

"No, we missed it. Can you believe it? It was on the same boulder as yesterday. Tell you about it when we meet up later. Do you think you're halfway around the hill?"

"Not a chance. We'll start back the way we came after staking out the next clearing. Probably will be about one thirty."

"Okay, good luck, out."

The voices over the radio woke the sleeping cat. Opening her eyes she looked toward the noise, but couldn't see anything. Shortly, she also heard movement. Listening, she watched the ground intently. She was still slightly uneasy, but her curiosity took over, anything moving was a potential meal. She wrapped her front paws around the trunk of the tree then placed her hind leg claws into the trunk, working her way down to the ground.

After emerging from a deer trail Eric observed, "This meadow looks a lot like the last one."

"Sure does. Let's find a good spot."

They worked their way along the west side of the meadow until they found a good location, only twenty yards from the trail. Eric set up the camouflage material differently this time, laying it over branches of an adjoining tree and wrapping it around the back so that only the front was open. Once they had the cover in place, they sat down and Buck made the first turkey call.

Immediately the cougar heard the sound and changed her direction. As she drew closer she slowed her pace, crouched and started to creep in to the turkey call.

About ten minutes later, "I think I hear quail on the far side, over there by that blackberry bush," Eric whispered pointing to the area.

"That would be a likely place for them. They are seed eaters and they especially like blackberry bushes. It provides cover to protect quail from the larger predators and also provides them with food when the berries are in season," Buck, ever the educator, answered.

"Other than the quail it's pretty dead out here. Too bad I missed," Eric lamented quietly.

"That's why you squeeze the trigger slowly instead of pulling it, squeezing the trigger keeps the barrel from pulling up."

"Thanks for the reminder."

"Life is full of learning experiences."

The cat slowly crept forward until she was right next to where the sound of the 'gobble, gobble' was originating. It couldn't be more than three feet from her but she couldn't understand why she couldn't see it. Glancing at the trees around her she was positive it must be on the ground. Patiently she sat there waiting for the next gobble or movement.

Softly Eric said, "We might as well head back. There's nothing going on here. Let's stop at the clearing where we saw the cougar before and have another try."

Buck gave another turkey call. The cat tensed.

"Okay, let's pack up and head out."

Eric made sure the safety was on before he rested his rifle against a log then stood up. As he started to grab the camouflage material he saw the cougar crouched down behind it.

"Holy crap!" as he jumped back and reached for his rifle.

The sudden appearance of a human startled the cat. Springing straight up from all fours the cat bolted.

Grabbing his rifle when he stood up, Buck turned around. Eric swung his rifle around too but in those few seconds the cat had already disappeared.

"Man that was close! I could have touched it when I was sitting down! I wonder how long it had been there?"

"Hard to tell, interesting though, it was right next to us but it didn't attack. Wonder why?" Buck queried.

"It probably couldn't see us. It heard the call but couldn't see anything. Probably was waiting for movement or a visual of the turkey. I'm sure it was expecting a turkey, not humans," Eric speculated.

"True, it's highly unlikely a cougar would attack two adults together. I think they only attack when they've scoped out the situation and completely understand what they're getting into. It wasn't expecting humans so we caught it by surprise when you stood up. That's why it bolted instead of attacking us."

Alarmed, Eric asked, "So who's hunting who here?"

"From now on I think we should sit back to back when we're doing the call from behind the camouflage. No sense tempting fate."

"Okay with me, that sounds like a good idea. That surprise about gave me a heart attack."

Soaring Eagle came straight down the hill to White Cloud. "You okay?" after checking him over.

"Yeah," a little unsteadily, "that was close though. Thanks for the warning. I had an uneasy feeling as I approached the boulder but when I didn't see anything up there I let down my guard a little. It must have been hiding in the branches that were over the side of the boulder."

"I could see two tails protruding from under the branches, moving slightly, but I was never able to see for sure where they were."

"So there were two of them again?" looking back up at the boulder, but seeing nothing.

"Yeah, the other one probably took off when I fired the shot."

Together they headed in the direction the cougar had escaped and continued comparing what they thought had happened.

"That's what I figured too. I didn't see anything on the boulder but the tails. I was just getting my binoculars focused on it when I saw the branches move. That's when I yelled."

"Good thing you did. It would have been on my back instead of me hitting it away with the rifle. Now that's an unpleasant thought."

"The other one is most likely long gone by now too," Soaring Eagle said.

"Probably, our attention was diverted so it had plenty of time to escape. Funny, it didn't attack also."

"Yeah, we'll have to do this a little differently tomorrow."

"Yep, I agree," said White Cloud.

Two hours later, after scouring the area for the attacker, Soaring Eagle said, "Amazing how they can disappear like that."

"We might as well head back to the rendezvous point. It'll be 3:30 by the time we get there."

Buck and Eric decided to go back to the other meadow where Eric had taken a shot at the cougar. They arrived there about 3:00.

"I think we should continue on to the place where we said we'd meet White Cloud and Soaring Eagle. We only have another half hour until rendezvous time. We're not going to have time to set up and wait here again."

"Okay by me. I'm getting tired."

"Yeah, I'm a little tired too."

Arriving first Buck and Eric stripped their packs off and sat down, resting against the packs. They each propped their rifle on their shoulder with the rifle butt on the ground.

"Hey, you guys look comfortable," White Cloud observed.

Startled, Eric looked up at Soaring Eagle only a few feet away, amazed he asked, "You did it again. I don't know how you can get up so close without us hearing you?"

"We're quiet, but it looked like you might have been snoozing," White Cloud said.

Now that everyone was together at the rendezvous point it was time to leave for their camp. No one really wanted to walk too far in the dark after all the cougar activity of the day. While walking each one took a turn in reliving their events of the day. The time passed quickly, and when they came upon the trail leading back to their campsite, it was early dusk. White Cloud took the lead then and about thirty minutes later they arrived at the meadow. Standing at the perimeter they watched the big bull elk grazing nearby.

"Pretty incredible that an elk is here in the vicinity of those cougars," Buck remarked. "I guess it's just one of those quirks in nature. They just haven't found it yet."

Once they arrived at the camp everyone was relieved to get their gear off. It had been a long day and the entire group was weary. Working as a team the evening preparation for dinner got started.

Eric immediately went about the task of setting up the kindling in tepee style in the fire pit, along with some dry pine needles to get the fire going. Soaring Eagle gathered some more wood while White Cloud fetched water from the stream. Buck went to the tree and lowered the food bag. No one spoke as each one tended to their chore at hand. Coming back from the stream White Cloud set the pan of water on top of the propane burner and lit it. Dinner wasn't far off and they all sat down to wait. Eric had the fire blazing away by then.

"Now that I've had some time to digest all of the happenings today I think we should come up with another plan," Buck sagely remarked.

"That's what Soaring Eagle and I were thinking."

The lone cougar had followed Buck and Eric and the two sisters had followed Soaring Eagle and White Cloud back to the rendezvous place. Shortly after the men joined up and began walking down the road together the three cougars, trailing them separately from a distance, sensed each other's presence and came together, shadowing the hunters back to their campsite.

The cats watched the men prepare for the night from a big old maple tree about one hundred yards away. They lost interest when the men sat down to eat dinner. At that time they left and returned to the area where they had slept earlier that morning. Swawa wasn't there so each cat got comfortable and quickly fell asleep.

Soaring Eagle asked, "Do you think we should all stay as a group tomorrow?"

"No, I don't think we should. We won't have any luck with all four us together," White Cloud replied.

"Eric and I have already discussed what we plan to do next time. We're going to sit back to back with the blinds on the sides. I figure it can't sneak up behind us that way."

"Maybe we shouldn't use the blind at all. It could still sneak up on the sides without us seeing it," Eric added.

"Possible, but it will likely see you a long time before you see it," Soaring Eagle stated.

"True, I'd rather see it when it's twenty to thirty yards away. Distance is better," Eric said.

"I agree," Buck threw in. "Okay we'll stick with the same plan tomorrow. Just be more cautious and aware of what's around us".

White Cloud spoke up, "Okay, that's good. Soaring Eagle, I think we should stay closer together tomorrow. Let's meet before we get to that large boulder and sneak in from there. Don't use the road, come in from the side. What do you think?"

"I think that's a good plan. What if there's no cougar at the boulder this time?" Soaring Eagle asked.

"Then I suggest we split up again and continue on to the top as we've been doing."

"Okay, that sounds reasonable to me," Soaring Eagle responded. "Let's go about ten minutes apart from there."

"Yeah, that sounds good."

The water was boiling and each one made up a freeze-dried dinner pack and returned to the fire pit area to eat.

Just noticing Eric said, "I don't see the elk anymore."

"He's probably moved on or found a place that's not in the open to lay down and digest whatever he's been eating," Soaring Eagle said.

By the time dinner was cleaned up it was nearly nine. Buck mentioned, "The temperature's dropping and its getting cold. I'm ready for bed anyway. This is it for me."

Soaring Eagle added, "Me too. It is getting cold out here."

White Cloud pulled the food bag back up high above the ground. Eric got some water from the stream and doused the fire.

By ten they were all snoring. Buck was snoring loud enough to draw the attention of the night creatures. A raccoon searched around the tents, stopping occasionally to listen to the buzz emanating from the thin walls separating the men from the elements. It continued over to the fire pit, trying to find any scrap of food the hunters might have left.

Shortly after midnight, hunger woke the kittens up. Swawa was still gone so the cats stretched and left the safety of the branches to hunt. They were all hungry enough to scavenge, but their sense of smell was not all that keen and yielded no results. Unaware of the raccoon nearby it was their keen hearing that brought the snoring to their attention. The peculiar sound drew the cats to the tents missing the raccoon by mere minutes.

The fast moving cold front was laden with moisture and it began snowing lightly. The falling snow buffered the night sounds, almost obliterating them. Undetected, the cats roamed around the tents. Remembering the previous experience they instinctively knew the hunters were inside. The largest cat gave a loud hiss quickly followed by a blood curdling scream from one of the others.

The men were jolted awake by the scream. White Cloud bolted upright and whispered, but loud enough for Buck to hear, "Did you hear that?"

Alarmed Eric responded, "Yeah."

Another scream.

Buck, slowly and as quietly as possible, unzipped his sleeping bag, "That sounded pretty close."

Two more screams in quick succession followed by another hiss.

"Don't move," warned White Cloud.

A tail slapped the side of his tent, causing snow to slide off the dome.

"It's snowing," he said softly to Soaring Eagle.

"I thought it might be. It's plenty cold."

They all reached for their rifles and as quiet as possible loaded a round, ready and waiting. There was no way they could shoot them this close to each other, unless one of the cats tore into the tent. There'd be no choice then.

After about thirty minutes of unsuccessful attempts to flush their prey out into the open the cats gave up and departed as silently as they had arrived.

Waiting an hour White Cloud said in a subdued voice, "I think they've given up."

"Was that cougars?" asked Eric.

"I'm pretty confident that it was."

"Man, I could've reached out and touched one if the tent hadn't been there," Eric said in awe.

"Their behavior is an enigma to me," White Cloud noted.

Settling down everyone slept fitfully for the rest of the night.

Photo by Lee Dygert

10

Just before daybreak they began getting up one by one.

"Dress warmly," Buck said to Eric, who was awake but hadn't made a move to get up yet. "Long underwear, gloves, and ski caps. We'll probably need it all today." He emerged from the tent to find White Cloud already outside looking around with his flashlight.

They discovered many cougar tracks in an inch of snow surrounding both tents. Eric exited the tent with a flashlight in hand and saw the prints right away. He sat back on this heals to get a closer look, "There are a lot of really good prints here."

"Hard to tell how many cougars there were," commented Soaring Eagle.

From what they could deduce the tracks were all close to the same size.

Soaring Eagle thought about what they had heard last night, the two screams almost together and a hiss. "I'd say three or more. These prints are not as big as I'd expect for full grown cougars. In fact, I can't find even one that appears to be adult size. This is really odd you know."

Continuing Soaring Eagle said, "The cougars we saw yesterday are probably the same ones that made these prints. I think they're a little young to be on their own. Speculating, I'd say maybe the mother got killed."

"Let's grab something we can eat on the way and get going. The tracks are still fresh," White Cloud said as he lowered the food bag.

As soon as the bag was down everyone quickly grabbed a couple of granola bars, dry biscuits, jerky, and some candy bars. White Cloud made sure everyone got plenty and asked Soaring Eagle to grab some items for him also. While the others were getting their backpacks on White Cloud hauled the food bag back up into the tree.

In the soft diffused light of sunrise, they made their way across the snow, following the tracks. Notably the tracks went in the same direction that they had hunted the past two days.

As they pressed on tracking the cats the snow began to melt more and more as the sun continued to rise higher in the sky. When they got to the base of the hill the prints had disappeared along with the melting snow.

Surprised Eric said, "This is weird. The tracks have led us right back to the base of the hill.

"I agree," White Cloud added, sitting down on a log. "It's almost as if they were leading us into a trap."

Incredulously Buck asked, "You think they're that smart?"

"Maybe, they're very smart animals," said Soaring Eagle.

"Hard for me to imagine they could come up with a plan like a trap," White Cloud commented. "They're smart, but not that smart. I don't think they're capable of reasoning. Maybe an ape or monkey could reason but not a cougar."

Eric spoke up, "I've seen shows on television where African lions work together to herd prey into a trap of waiting lions."

"African lions are pride animals. They've been working together for generations. In Africa there are huge plains with animal herds. There's lots of food for them there. This area is totally different. I've never read anything about this kind of behavior in cougars or mountain lions."

"Maybe we should stay together considering our visitors last night," White Cloud added. "They obviously know we're here. Maybe they're watching us right now."

Buck replied, "One already made an attempt to attack you so we know they mean business."

"I think you're right, let's go up the hill together."

White Cloud and Soaring Eagle led side by side with Buck and Eric following behind about ten yards. Each had their rifle loaded, safety on, and resting in the crook of their arm.

Approaching the area of the big boulder White Cloud said, "Let's spread out here. Soaring Eagle and I will go up the hill and work our way, side by side, toward the boulder. We've been here before so we know the terrain and trails. You two stay on the road, side by side. The boulder is about ten minutes away still. You'll actually see it the last thirty yards. Stay on the down hill side of the road, well away from the boulder and have your rifles ready. Give us ten minutes head start then take your time. It'll provide us with ample time to view the boulder and watch for any signs of movement. We'll stay east of the boulder just in case you see them and get a chance for a shot. Make sure you shoot only toward the west or north."

"Okay. Good luck and be careful."

A small game trail was located and they hiked up the hill via the trail. Brush was touching them at the waist as they ascended, but also concealing them to some degree as they advanced.

Buck and Eric sat on a rock at the side of the road watching them go up the hill and eventually disappear from their sight. Eric checked his watch and said, "It's been ten minutes."

"Okay, let's go."

"Think we'll see them?"

"Considering the events of the last two days I'd say it's highly likely. It's quite possible they're watching us right now."

They made their way slowly up the road keeping a watchful eye, both ahead and behind them. It wasn't long before they could see the boulder up ahead. Indeed, it did look like a good hideout for a cougar to lay in wait for prey to simply pass below. No cougar could be seen but Buck noticed the evergreen branches covering the east end of the boulder. Eric stopped and took his binoculars out to get a better look.

"Take a close look at those branches on the right side of the boulder," Buck suggested. "That's where the one was hiding when White Cloud was attacked.

"Not a thing. Nothing that even resembles a cougar, the color of tan or any movement."

"Stay here and keep an eye on the boulder, I'll walk on up ahead." Buck took the safety off and held the rifle at the ready as he advanced.

The cougar kittens slept until nearly seven the next morning. When they woke up, they discovered that

Swawa was back, but asleep. Yesterday's events of following the men during the day, and later to the campsite, with an unsuccessfully attempt to flush them out in the night led them to develop a different hunting strategy. This time they stuck together and stalked from a distance. Slinking along in the brush they remained unobtrusive watching the two men.

Buck passed in front of the boulder. When nothing happened, he yelled to White Cloud and Soaring Eagle, "Do you see anything?"

"Nothing here," White Cloud answered.

Buck could hear him but he couldn't see either of them.

He called back to Eric, "See anything Eric?"

"Nope," he yelled back. "Nothing at all."

White Cloud and Soaring Eagle came down the slope to the boulder and searched around. White Cloud looked down at Buck and said, "Nothing here."

The men all joined together on the road by the boulder. White Cloud scratched his head in wonder, "Well, they're not here today."

"Maybe they just outsmarted us," Soaring Eagle remarked. "They may not be on the boulder but that doesn't mean they're not around. They're creatures of habit, if they were here two days in a row and we're here now, it's a good bet they're somewhere near."

Glancing around they all tried to find what they thought would be a good cougar hiding place. There were plenty of possibilities, but nothing seemed obvious or stood out as a likely place.

"Let's go on up to the top of the hill in pairs," suggested White Cloud. "Give us a fifteen minute head start. It's less than thirty minutes to the top from here. We'll check over the side above the boulder to see if there's any activity when we pass above it."

"Okay, we'll see you at the top then," said Buck.

Eric sat down on a large rock at the low side of the road while Buck removed the round from the chamber and put it back in the clip. Still scouting the area suddenly Eric said, "I think I see something moving in the brush down the road."

Buck turned to look. Eric pointed, "There, in the brush."

Buck started walking, "Let's go have a look."

Eric followed as they headed toward the suspicious area. They both held up their rifles approaching the spot.

"Nothing here," Buck observed.

Eric looked all around and down the hill. There were plenty of bushes large enough for a cougar to hide in, no trees close by though.

Buck looked at his watch and asked, "Shall we head up the hill? It's about that time."

"Sure. There's nothing here. Maybe it was a small animal like a rabbit."

When Buck and Eric went around the bend on the way up the hill, the cats crossed the road and went straight up the side. Conveniently, there was a large maple tree and all three cats climbed up and immediately flattened themselves against big branches about twenty feet off the ground. The cats hunkered down and watched every move Buck and Eric made as they walked up the road.

Unaware of the cougars' presence Buck and Eric passed right under the tree. Once the men were out of sight again the three cats dropped down from the tree and quickly found a game trail that paralleled the road.

Eric called out a greeting when they caught up to White Cloud and Soaring Eagle. They had been sitting on a fallen tree at a clearing where the road seemed to end.

"See anything?" asked Soaring Eagle.

Eric shook his head, "Nothing."

"How long have you two been here?" Buck asked.

"Fifteen, maybe twenty minutes," White Cloud answered.

Bravely Soaring Eagle announced, "I think I'll go back down the road alone. Let's try the decoy method again. Only stay about ten minutes behind me this time White Cloud." Not waiting for an answer he continued, "A little measure of safety so I'd recommend that Buck and Eric follow together about ten minutes behind White Cloud."

Buck asked, "Do you think that's a good idea? There could be two or three cougars out there and together."

"I think it's highly unlikely we'll see any with four of us together. Even with two people together it's probably a long shot."

"If you say so, I guess it's okay with me," Buck replied.

Eric added, "Me too."

"Go ahead and head out. I'll follow you in ten minutes. That'll give Buck and Eric twenty minutes to rest up."

Soaring Eagle rose and put his backpack on. As he started down the road he chambered a round and put the safety on, carrying the rifle in the crook of his right arm.

"At least it's warmed up a bit," White Cloud said, "but it's unfortunate the snow melted, tracking is a lot easier in the snow."

"Yeah, it's a bummer. I was sure we were going to get one this morning," Eric responded, disappointed.

White Cloud added, "The day is not over yet. See you at the bottom of the hill." Lifting his backpack to his shoulder he cradled the rifle across his chest, the barrel pointing up over the left shoulder.

Ten minutes later Buck and Eric stood up. Buck asked, "Ready?"

"You bet," was the stimulated response.

The three cougar sisters zeroed in on the lone hunter as soon as he came around the first bend in the road. Hunger had driven the kittens to desperate measures and the solitary human presented an opportunity to solve their problem. Instead of following him they went straight down the hill to the road below him and waited.

Soaring Eagle knew he was the decoy and that he needed to be very careful. Walking slower than usual, he searched both sides of the road ahead of him. He paid more attention to the sounds around him than he would have under normal circumstances, knowing he was in a dangerous situation.

Well concealed behind bushes the cougars were tense but patiently waiting. They pressed themselves down low to the ground to stay hidden, but ready to spring.

As soon as Soaring Eagle was directly in front of the bushes the cats muscles rippled, their tails twitching rapidly. The bushes were in close proximity, literally surrounding them, and one of the tails brushed ever so slightly up against the leaves and made a whisper of a noise.

Every little noise was a possible warning signal. When Soaring Eagle heard the bushes move he whirled around at the slight sound. An automatic reflex he had his rifle lowered and directed toward the sound clicking the safety off.

His quick response startled the kittens. They crouched down even lower and kept their tails still.

Soaring Eagle looked directly at the bushes the cougars were behind, but did not see anything. After scanning the immediate area for a couple of minutes he was satisfied that it was nothing, thinking that perhaps a breeze was the cause of the rustling branches or maybe a small animal moving around. Resuming his journey alone he kept looking back over his shoulder every few steps.

When the hunter was out of sight again the cougars moved down the hill. They jumped onto the boulder, then down onto the road below, crossing over to the lower side then went down past the next bend. They soon found a big old maple tree with huge branches that would serve as a good observation point and provide concealment.

A sudden rush of fear washed over Soaring Eagle, then quickly ebbed as he approached the boulder. His rifle at the ready, the safety off, he was twenty yards away and had a good view of the boulder from the low side of the road. Sweat dripped off his brow. There wasn't anything obvious so he continued slowly on past the boulder, his senses on full alert. Thirty yards down the road from the boulder relief washed over him and he put the safety back on. Another ten minutes passed and he had a sudden urge to urinate. Stopping at the side of the road, he propped his rifle against the trunk of a large maple tree. He removed his pack, placing it next to the rifle. Standing at the lower edge of the road looking down the hill, he mumbled, "Ah."

Cougars will sometimes observe animal prey for long periods of time waiting for the right moment to move in for the kill. An animal relieving itself presents a prime opportunity for an attack. The cougar knows instinctively that the prey cannot react as fast as it would under other circumstances.

Soaring Eagle was directly under the three cats. One of the kittens sprang from the tree and landed right on Soaring Eagle's back. Her jaws latched onto his head and she ripped the scalp off from the middle of his forehead back to the neck in a matter of seconds.

"Ahhh!" screamed Soaring Eagle. Desperately he thrashed about trying to fling the cougar off. Her claws were firmly imbedded in his shoulder, forearm, and the back of his legs. Continuing to scream hoping that White Cloud would hear him he tried in vain to reach the 9mm in his shoulder holster. The claws held fast and he was barely able to move his right arm. He then struggled with his left hand trying to get his knife on the other side. Searing pain shot down both legs as the cougar raked her claws through his pants, tearing away the cloth, gashing in and out the flesh as the cloth tore away. She tasted fresh, warm blood and longed for more.

Soaring Eagle knew he was in big trouble and spun around with all his might, dislodging the cat, but it raked its claws over his shoulder and down his back as it tumbled off. Stunned, but still standing Soaring Eagle faced the cat and reached for his 9mm. Just as he was pulling it out of the holster the cat sprang toward him. Protectively he held up his left arm knowing the cat was going for his throat. She locked on to his arm with her jaws and with her hind legs clawed into his thighs.

As soon as White Cloud heard the first scream he ran as fast as possible. When he first saw Soaring Eagle, thirty yards away, they were too entwined for him to get off a shot at it. He continued to run toward them. Soaring Eagle was flat on his back with the cat madly trying to get at his throat when he arrived. The cat was totally focused on the attack when White Cloud ran up from behind.

They were too close together for him to try to shoot the cougar on Soaring Eagle's back so he dropped his rifle and pulled his knife out. Jumping into the attack from behind the cat he stabbed it with all of his might right between the shoulder blades. Pulling the knife out for another stab the cat wheeled around and lunged at him. White Cloud thrust his left fist directly into its mouth and down the throat as far as he could. The shocked cougar went into spasmodic convulsions, claws flying trying to get free. White Cloud thrust the knife again into the cat's upper chest three times in rapid succession as the cougar continued to thrash about trying to get claws into him. Finally, he thrust his knife into the cougar's throat, slashing to the left, severing the juggler vein. The cougar reacted trying to get away, muscles slowly beginning to relax as White Cloud pushed it off to his left side. The cat took two steps and collapsed.

The smell of fresh blood in the air brought the two sisters leaping out of the tree to the ground behind White Cloud. Buck and Eric came running around the bend just as the cougars hit the ground.

"Look out White Cloud!" Buck and Eric yelled in unison.

One of the cats landed on White Cloud's backpack and the other went to the left side. They ran toward White Cloud and Eric dropped his pack as Buck reached White Cloud. Buck was able to place the muzzle of his rifle against the side of the cougar's chest and pulled the trigger, blasting the cat off of White Cloud. It landed flat on the ground, unmoving with a large hole in the side where the bullet exited the chest.

Eric dropped down on his right knee, using the left knee as a tripod he rested his left elbow on the knee and pointed his rifle at the remaining cat as it retreated. The cougar bolted across the road for the downhill slope moving fast. He had a clear shot, and without hesitation, Eric's reaction was swift and sure. He squeezed the trigger hitting it in the left shoulder. It rolled over the side of the road and jumped up, Eric squeezed the trigger again hitting it in the upper part of the left front leg. It somersaulted in mid air and landed on its back with a thump, unmoving. Eric knelt there watching it for a minute to make sure it didn't get back up.

White Cloud had teeth puncture wounds in his left forearm and some scratch wounds on his right arm. He was slightly dazed. Buck took a good look at him, but he said, "Get Soaring Eagle, I'll be okay."

Eric got to Soaring Eagle first. Seeing the scalp laying next to him he immediately assessed the damage. There were gouges all over his body and he was unconscious. Eric took off his own jacket and shirt, then removed his T-shirt and began tearing it into four large strips. By then Buck was kneeling at Soaring Eagle's side checking for a pulse.

"He's got a weak pulse, probably in shock. Soaring Eagle, can you hear me?" There was no response.

Eric was pressing his T-shirt pieces against the largest wounds to stop the bleeding and talking to him, "Soaring Eagle, hang on, you're going to be okay. Don't give up, hang on!"

Buck got the first aid kit out of his pack and began applying antibiotic spray to the many wounds. He applied gauze and tape to the larger ones but didn't have enough to cover all the wounds.

White Cloud stumbled over to them. "Is he alive?"

Buck's quick reply, "Yes, but we've got to get him to a hospital fast. I think he's in shock and he's lost a lot of blood."

Buck removed his backpack and dug out his cell phone, "No reception. Damn!"

When Eric had the bleeding stopped he said, "I think if we can make a stretcher we'll be able to carry him back to the cars a lot faster. I'll go see what I can find."

Buck got some rope from his pack and told White Cloud to stay with Soaring Eagle. "Keep talking to him. Eric and I are going to make a stretcher."

"Okay," he said placing his hand on Soaring Eagle's chest.

"Hang on old friend. We'll get you out of here." He reached over and picked up his scalp. After inspecting it, he took out his water bottle and rinsed off the inside then squirted some water on Soaring Eagles head to rinse some of the dirt off. Satisfied that it appeared clean enough he placed it back on Soaring Eagle's head as carefully as he could. He moved it around a little to make it fit back into place. "You'll be okay."

It took over ten minutes for Eric to find a large enough and suitable branch. The same tree yielded a second branch and Eric quickly hacked away at it. Dragging both branches back to Buck he found his dad unraveling the rope. They removed the smaller branches and cut off the end of one to make them a uniform length a little over six feet long. Laying the limbs down about 18 inches apart Buck lashed the rope to each side and weaved it back and forth creating a crossed loop at each side of the stretcher. He worked quickly, but it took about a half hour to complete.

Carefully they laid it down next to Soaring Eagle. Buck took Soaring Eagle's shoulders, cradling his head between his forearms and Eric lifted his feet.

White Cloud straddled Soaring Eagle and tugged on his belt to lift him up and over onto the stretcher.

Buck and Eric put their backpacks on while White Cloud checked for a pulse again, "He's still got a pulse but he hasn't moved at all."

"Eric and I will carry him. You grab the rifles. I don't think it would be a good idea to leave them here. We'll have to come back anyway to pick up the camping equipment and other packs tomorrow."

"I'm pretty sure I can carry all the rifles but not my pack too," he said putting a rifle over each shoulder and carrying the other two in the crook of his arms.

Eric grabbed the head end of the stretcher and led the way. Buck said, "Let's take the road to the cutoff, where we came in the other day. It's not the most direct way, but it'll be faster than cutting through the woods."

Twenty minutes later Eric said, "Let's rest a minute."

"Good idea," Buck agreed as he put the stretcher down. He checked Soaring Eagle's pulse once again.

Touching Soaring Eagle's cheek, Buck spoke with confidence, "Soaring Eagle, we're almost to the car. Hang in there you're going to be okay."

Soaring Eagle opened one eye slightly. It was unseeing and had a far away gaze, then it slowly closed.

After seeing his eye open they were all encouraged and felt new energy. Eric said, "Let's go!" and he picked up the stretcher handles.

"How are you doing White Cloud?" Buck asked, picking up his end of the stretcher.

"I'm ready, I'll make it," in a weak voice. He struggled with his load of rifles.

White Cloud walked along beside the stretcher with his right hand on Soaring Eagle's hand, "Hang on old friend, don't give up. It won't be long now."

They left the road and went north on the trail they had used to get to the meadow and campsite on the first day. White Cloud had to drop back behind Buck when they left the road. The ground was flat and the trail was wide enough for them to carry the stretcher, but it was slow going because of the weight they were carrying. An hour later they spotted the SUV and this gave them renewed strength.

Setting the stretcher down on the ground Buck unlocked the rear door of the SUV. To make enough room for Soaring Eagle he lay down the seats in the back. White Cloud placed the rifles on the floor under the folded rear seats and then took the head end and Eric took the feet and placed Soaring Eagle in the back. Buck pulled while they pushed the stretcher in, but the back door wouldn't close. As careful as possible they rolled Soaring Eagle off the stretcher and took it out leaving it at the side of the road.

"Eric, you drive, I'll stay back here with Soaring Eagle," Buck said.

"Me too," White Cloud said climbing in the back.

He placed his hand on Soaring Eagle's shoulder and reassuringly said, "Hang in there old friend. We're in the car now. It won't be much longer before we're at the hospital."

Soaring Eagle slowly opened both eyes and looked at White Cloud, over to Buck, then back at White Cloud before closing them again.

"Hang on Soaring Eagle, don't let go." Buck urged Eric, "Let's go son, easy over the rough road."

Eric wanted to floor it but his dad was right, the road was too rough and even at 10 MPH it still seemed too fast. It took thirty minutes just to get to the highway but once on it Eric pressed the gas peddle to the floor. Sailing down the road as fast as he could safely go, slowing only for the curves. Leaving the base of the mountains they were in Arlington when White Cloud pointed out the street for the hospital. They were all relieved when Eric pulled up to the emergency room entrance.

Honking the horn and slamming on the brakes they made their presence known. Two attendants came running out to the SUV and another followed with a gurney. Buck jumped out to open the back door for the attendants. One of them took a cursory look to assess the needs, "Whoa, what happened to him?"

White Cloud told him, "Cougar attack."

"Any back or spinal injuries that you know of?"

Buck reported, "No, but we carried him on a makeshift stretcher for about two hours, to get him to the car, and he hasn't regained consciousness since the attack that we know of."

The three attendants worked him carefully onto the gurney and whisked him away, his scalp still raggedly attached to the top of his head.

Another nurse came up to White Cloud to get information on Soaring Eagle but took one look at him and said, "You look like you could use some assistance also."

"Probably, I'll need some antibiotics for sure," he responded.

She led the three of them to a treatment room and took all the information she needed for both White Cloud and Soaring Eagle. Another nurse joined them about half an hour later and cleaned the numerous scratch wounds, bandaged him up and returned with a prescription for antibiotics.

A young woman parted the curtains and walked in. "Are you the friends of the man that was attacked by the cougar?"

"Yes," they all responded.

"I'm Dr. Tenaka, Soaring Eagle is going to be okay. It took a lot of stitches. We were able to reattach his scalp but had to cut off some of the skin edges. Good thing you placed it back on his head. It gave it enough blood flow to keep it viable. We had to give him two pints of blood because of the blood loss. Actually, he's very lucky to be alive. He opened his eyes periodically and he was able to squeeze my hand when I told him he was in the hospital."

"Can we see him now?" White Cloud asked.

"I think it would be best to wait until tomorrow. He's still very weak."

Photo by Lee Dygert

11

Swawa awoke just after dark. She had not seen her kittens for two days and could tell they had not returned during the night. She emerged from the concealment of the tree branches and gave a short cry. Hearing no response she began roaming their familiar trails, giving a short cry periodically trying to locate her kittens. She roamed the trails coming upon the human's campsite around three in the morning. Sniffing all around she felt that her kittens had been there. She continued her search for her kittens into the early morning hours.

Around ten she came upon two of the kittens laying in the road. She studied each one closely, licking their faces. One at a time she picked them up by the scruff of their neck, gently shook it then laid it back down. Letting out a loud shriek of pain she knew they were dead. Continuing to inspect their bodies and licking their faces she paced the area for twenty minutes and then set out to look for the third one.

Nearly an hour later she found it and repeated the process of licking its face and picking it up. Again, there was no response. This time she lay down against her kitten and fell asleep.

The next morning Buck and Eric picked up White Cloud at his house on the way in to the hospital. Buck greeted him, "How are you feeling?"

"I ache all over, but I'll live."

"Think you'll be able to make it back in there to retrieve the tent and stuff?"

"Yeah no problem."

At the hospital they were led to the intensive care ward. White Cloud took Soaring Eagle's hand in both of his and said, "Soaring Eagle, it's White Cloud." Soaring Eagle opened his eyes.

"How are you feeling?"

"Drugged," he responded in a weak voice, squeezing White Cloud's hand back. "Lots of pain so they're keeping me doped up." His eyes closed again.

The charge nurse came in, "He doesn't stay conscious very long at a time, but he should be much better by tomorrow."

"Thanks," White Cloud said, then to Buck he said, "We might as well head up the hill and get our stuff. I'll come back here and stay the night with him. I'm feeling a lot better now than I was yesterday."

"Yeah, we need to get our cougars too," Eric announced.

On the way out to Buck's SUV in the parking lot White Cloud said, "The meat won't be any good by now, but we should take the heads and pelts to the Fish and Wildlife station for examination. They take a bunch of measurements, the teeth will tell them how old the cats were, maybe if they're related. They keep a lot of statistical information. They'll give us the pelts back in a few days."

They pulled out of the hospital parking lot and headed up the mountain. Buck said, "We'll stop on our way back too and check on Soaring Eagle. He seems to be a lot better today."

"The hunting regulations pamphlet says we have to turn in the head and pelt within three days. I imagine they might be interested in the story too."

Buck pulled up next to White Cloud's truck and announced, "Here we are." Eric and White Cloud had been napping during the ride out to the woods, in spite of the bumpy road.

As they got out Buck spied the stretcher they'd left and said, "We might as well use this stretcher to carry the pelts out."

They each put on backpacks, mostly empty, except for water bottles, some snack food, rifle shell and a first aid kit in Buck's. They all slung the rifles over their shoulder. Buck then picked up one end of the stretcher.

"Those pelts will get heavy, especially three," and White Cloud picked up the other end.

Eric took off in the lead heading for the meadow. It was becoming a familiar trail now and the hike to the campsite went quickly.

"Looks just like it did when we left yesterday morning," Eric had observed.

"Yeah, cougar tracks and all," Buck said studying a print near the fire pit.

White Cloud and Eric both took a look. "Looks bigger than the ones we saw yesterday morning," White Cloud observed.

"That's what I was thinking," added Buck.

Checking the campsite area for additional prints and for any other signs in the immediate area and in the trees there was nothing that they could find. Buck said, "We might as well head out. It's nearly noon and we need to get to the packs and skin the cougars. I'd like to get back to the car before dark."

Eric inquired, "How long does it take to skin a cougar?"

White Cloud answered, "It depends on how careful you want to be. I've never skinned one before, but based on skinning deer and elk I'd say forty minutes to maybe an hour."

Buck commented, "It's been a long time since I skinned a deer so I imagine it'll take me a bit longer."

Eric was pumped about the idea, "Well, I've never skinned anything."

"You can watch me," White Cloud instructed. "You'll get the hang of it pretty fast."

It took them about an hour to get everything loaded in their packs from the campsite. Buck had brought along two compact entrenching tools to bury the carcasses and placed them on the top of his pack. "Ready," Buck said shouldering the much heavier pack.

"Let's go!" both Eric and White Cloud said together.

Suddenly Swawa woke up to noise on the road above her. There were some bushes nearby and she darted behind them for cover, looking up at the road. Three men carrying rifles approached and stopped at her two kittens lying in the road. Knowing this development meant danger, she quietly slipped away. Once she knew she was well out of their sight she ran non-stop for twenty minutes until she collapsed at the base of a large cedar tree and fell into an exhausted sleep.

Buck and Eric watched as White Cloud began to skin the cat he had killed, showing them how to do it. "You start at the anus and cut up the underside of the belly to the base of the chin with a shallow incision just under the skin. Then the center line cut up each leg to the paw then slice the paw off at the end of the tibia and fibula. Remove the head at the top of the neck by slicing between the vertebrae."

"Well, you were right it's less than an hour. Let's go retrieve the one you shot Eric. We'll do them all here so it's easier to bury the remains in one place."

Buck and Eric carried the other cougar up the hill to where White Cloud was skinning the second one. "Well this is your cat Eric so you can skin it," Buck said.

Getting down on his knees, Eric went to work, slowly working the knife as instructed.

"This is the one you shot Buck. Do you want to finish it up?"

"I was sort of thinking that you and Soaring Eagle would each want one. We don't really need two of them at our house."

Nearly finished with the job White Cloud said, "Okay by me, thanks."

Buck laid the first pelt on the stretcher. He then took the entrenching tool from his pack and began digging a hole at the side of the road bed. White Cloud put the pelt he just finished on the stretcher and watched Eric for a few minutes and asked, "Do you need some help?"

"No, not yet anyway. I'm not as fast as you but I can do it."

By the time Eric finished and put the pelt on top of the other two Buck and White Cloud had the two carcasses in the pit. Eric carried his over and they buried them all together.

"There's a good chance scavengers will find them and dig them up. Not much goes to waste out here in the woods," White Cloud said.

"Well at least we did the right thing and buried them," Eric replied.

In his native language, White Cloud said something over the grave. To Buck and Eric he explained, "I said my father is now avenged. I'm just glad Soaring Eagle didn't get killed in the process."

"Amen," Buck finished the unusual ceremony.

Buck grabbed the lead end of the stretcher and White Cloud took the back. Eric followed behind. White Cloud looked over his shoulder at Eric and asked," Are you going to go cougar hunting again?"

Thinking about Soaring Eagle, he said, "Probably not, I think one trip is going to be enough. I'll probably go deer hunting with Jeremiah though."

The three men quietly walked into Soaring Eagle's hospital room, White Cloud went up to the bed and gently touched his friend's arm in one of the few places that didn't have a bandage.

"Soaring Eagle."

Soaring Eagle opened both eyes and looked directly at his friend, "Hi," in a very weak voice. "How long have I been here?"

"About 24 hours, we brought you in last night."

"You look a lot better today," Buck remarked.

"My head really hurts."

Concerned White Cloud asked, "Do you need us to get the nurse?"

"No, they just gave me a pain pill. It should take effect soon."

Eric asked, "Have you looked in the mirror yet?"

"Yeah, the nurse had me look a little while ago. Guess that's why my head hurts so much. My hair will likely fall out but the doctor said once it's completely healed the hair should grow back."

Soaring Eagle laid there in amazement as White Cloud told him everything that had happened yesterday. Eric told him about the skinning and burying the carcasses today.

"Thanks for getting me out of there. The doctor and nurses said they weren't sure I was going to make it when they got a good look at me in the emergency room. Maybe five or six more days here as long as the infection doesn't get worse. This IV has antibiotics in it but they have to change most of my dressings three or four times a day to keep the infection from getting out of control. They said cougar bites, and the scratch wounds from the claws create serious infections. They carry a lot of germs, especially in the claws. I'll probably have to be on antibiotics for over a month."

White Cloud offered, "I'm going to stay here for the night and keep you company. Do you need anything?"

"No."

Starting for the door, Buck said, "Guess we'll head out. We'll be back to see you in a couple of days. I'll take the heads and pelts to the Department of Fish and Wildlife station tomorrow. When they're done getting the information they need I'll go back and pick up the pelts."

Eric phoned home on the cellular phone to let his mom know they would be home soon, probably in twenty minutes.

Using the garage door opener when they pulled into the driveway Robert was in the garage anxiously waiting. He watched as Buck and Eric got the pelts out of the car and laid them on a tarp.

Buck took one side of the tarp and Eric the other and together got it up on his workbench. Robert carefully studied the head first, taking in every detail, the size of the teeth, the tongue stretched out to the side, eyes open, staring, unseeing. Putting his hand next to the paw he was surprised at how large the paw was and how powerful it looked. He spent an hour going over the whole pelt, the bullet holes down to the tip of the tails. It was an awesome sight, three cougar hides laid side by side.

In the middle of the night, a week later, Swawa stood on top of the boulder. She let out one blood curdling scream after another. She was in heat once again.

References and suggested reading

The Beast in the Garden, 2003, David Baron

Cat Attacks, 2001, Jo Deurbrouck & Dean Miller

Cougar, 1999, Harold P. Danz

Cougar Attacks, Encounters of the Worst Kind, 2001, Kathy Etling

Cougar Hunt, 2000, J.R. Stoddard

Track of the Cat, 1997, Maurice Hornocker, PhD